DUST ON THEIR

HEARTS

by

Carolena Torres

"When the dust of Mexico falls upon
your heart, you will never be the same."

Front cover photograph
by Maria Di Paola Blum

Front and back cover design
by Luis Mancera McCormick
photogenesisajijic@yahoo.com

Book format by Betty L. Wright
blw@blwbookworks.com

Ajijic, Mexico

Printed by
Groppe Libros, Guadalajara, MX

TABLE OF CONTENTS

BERNICE

MARGARET

LINDA

PREFACE

"DUST ON THEIR HEARTS" is fiction. It began as an entertaining idea at a Sunday brunch in a small B & B in Mexico, and was first shared with a group of lively vacationers, all very willing listeners.

My story line began when this wonderful collection of tourists, all strangers to each other, bonded in a small town on the banks of Lake Chapala over an extended courtyard brunch. We met on our vacations for several years afterward. As I invented more characters and expanded on the story, we discussed it, and laughed together. Wherever they are now, I hope they remember.

My story base began then and though the names and faces of my friends have changed over the years, the story went on in my head. More characters developed with the dust of Mexico on their hearts.

These descriptive sketches of my characters are all imaginary, and I hope they will help you to see in your mind's eye an image of a place, a person, a family and their lives and loves.

The small village, the restaurant and the motel do not exist. Lake Chapala, however, is nearby to the setting and has had a colorful history for many hundreds of years. A variety of small villages grew around the lake banks when fishing in its mysterious waters satisfied the livelihood of generations of anglers.

I give my wholehearted thanks to Neill James for making popular the saying, "When once the dust of Mexico has settled upon your heart, you cannot find peace in any other land."

Areas may be recognizable and some events just might have happened.

BERNICE

Chapter 1

SUNDAY BRUNCH – 1980

LAKE CHAPALA, MEXICO

Bernice watched the gray-black pavement roll
by through a dinner plate sized hole in the floor of the
rickety yellow bus. From long practice she
automatically avoided the opening, instead stepping
down heavily from the Mexican autobus and picking
her way across cobblestones. She was hungry and her
stomach was grumbling. She passed under the unruly
blaze of red and orange bougainvillea massed over a
rusty iron arch. Every Sunday after church was the
bountiful brunch at El Gallo Loco (The Crazy Rooster)
and her mouth was moist in anticipation. Crossing the
familiar flagstone patio past dozens of flourishing green

and fragrant herb filled pots, and tables of other diners, she settled with a deep sigh at her favorite side of the worn plank table and appreciated the shade of a lacy lavender jacaranda tree. This was like her second home as she had been enjoying the friendly service and comfortable atmosphere for over twelve years. Next door, and sharing a circular driveway was the Casa Redondo, (Round House) a five room motel that was once a stable. Both buildings at one time were a part of a proud, very old hacienda that had been abandoned for over fifty years. Memories of a flourishing community lingered in songs and old men's stories. The main house was some distance away, and its roofless, crumbling walls, because of some long forgotten person's decision became the choice for weekend street markets, musicians and attendant food carts. The barn had been restored and remodeled and was a perfect setting for the restaurant. The Brunch at the El Gallo Loco (The Crazy Rooster) was first a pleasure, most of all an indulgence. Each Sunday Brunch was complimented by a long standing practice of free margueritas. It was a week after Easter, and the contrast of the pale pink primavera and purple jacaranda was a lovely setting for the start of another enjoyable day. Her friend Maigret was already there.

"Hola Bernie, how are you?"

"Hello Maigret, you know what they say; another day above ground is a good one for me. What have you been up to today?"

"I brought cakes for the Brunch, and a customer is picking up a birthday cake here that I baked for her son's party, so as long as I am here, thought I would treat myself."

Bernie reached down into her bag and quickly changed into a pair of battered slippers. "I need a treat too. Some days I really feel my age. It's time for an unbirthday present. I need a margarita quick, maybe two."

"You're not old Bernie, you're classic!" Laughing, they both looked up at the same time to see a blond young woman hesitating in the open door of the restaurant, her eyes darting from table to table, finding no open seat.

Bernie's eyes held on the young girl in the doorway: a mass of blond curls piled high on her head, white tube top, black culottes, huge red purse and matching red sling back shoes. "Ain't she a picture? If you are looking for a seat honey, it's the only one left," waving her hand to the bench across the table. "It's better outside, come on over."

With a weak smile, the blond curls started toward them, red high heels clicking across the flagstones. Stumbling, she dropped onto the bench. "Oh, thanks a bunch. I'm here all by myself and don't know anyone. I'm Linda Lou, Linda Lou Campbell. I'm staying over there at the motel across the yard for a while."

Bernie held her hand out across the table, "I'm Bernie Davis Walters, and this here is Margaret Stern, we call her Maigret. We go way back. We were neighbors in Long Beach, that's California, and we lived next door to each other until after her son was born. We came down on the same plane together. My, that must have been twelve or thirteen years ago."

With a grateful smile, Linda took her hand, "Pleased to meet you, I'm sure. It sure feels good to be somewhere. I hardly slept all night; I had so much on my mind. It's terrible when you don't have anyone to talk to about big decisions. You know like a mother, or a friend."

Maigret touched Linda's hand, "You can talk to us, and we are all friends here."

A tall, dark haired waiter appeared with a large frosty pitcher of pink margaritas on a tray and three long stemmed glasses. "On the house ladies; all you can drink… it comes with the brunch. Whenever you are ready, serve yourself from the buffet."

Bernie raised her brimming glass, "Cheers, bottoms up and all that."

Linda Lou looked intently at her rosy hued glass. "I never drank a mar-gar-eet."

Letting the delicious liquid flow over her tongue, Bernie sighed, "Go on gal, it will brighten your day…and it's a mar-gar-eet-tah."

"My day, my week, my life – all of it sure needs brightening. Here goes. Oh! It tastes like punch, icy punch." She took another swallow, then another and another. "This is really good, and I am so thirsty. I just got in late last night and will be staying at the Casa Redondo until my money runs out I guess, or until I get a job. Is there any kind of work around here?"

Maigret's eyes met Bernie's, and then she looked back at Linda and said carefully, "All I know is that it would have to be a very special job. What do you do?

"I've been a model and I've been in beauty pageants, but I don't want to do that anymore." Covering her face with her hands she continued, "I really don't want to go back. A terrible thing happened; it was my boyfriend that did it. Do you think a person can live with his privates cut off?"

Maigret stared at Linda and stuttered, "Did you...have you...are you in trouble?"

Linda shook her head, "Oh no, I didn't do it, I just wish I had. He deserved it. What kind of work do you do?" Maigret explained that she was a baker working out of her home, a casita which was a small house in Bernie's back yard.

Linda sighed, "I don't cook much but I know how to clean house. How long have you lived here? Is this a good town? Why did you pick this place? I mean it, I am never going back. Oh, I already said that."

Maigret closed her eyes and sipped the cool drink. Settling into a comfortable position she replied, "One question at a time. Bernie and I came from the states about a dozen years ago and found this restaurant and became friends with the owner. We both fell in love with Mexico and it feels like home to us. The people are wonderful and the weather is always just right. There is a saying here that 'When the dust of Mexico falls upon your heart, you will never be the same' and I really believe that."

Bernie finished chewing a mouthful of Eggs Benedict, enjoying to the fullest the tangy lemon sauce lavishly crowning the poached eggs perched on top of the ham slice and crusty muffin. Wiping her mouth, she spoke thoughtfully, "I have a good life here. I had a good job in the Army. I've been a lot of places and done a lot of things…don't regret any of them. There are good memories and some sad ones. Being a nurse in the war is a ringside seat for tragedy. Looking back, I wouldn't change my life. I think the best part has been living here. It's an interesting story of how I just answered an ad for a job and ended up here."

Chapter 2

OPERATION TORCH

NORTH AFRICA - 1942

It was November 8, 1942. With knowledge and assistance from Great Britain, The United States was invading North Africa somewhere near Arzen, Algeria, in a three-pronged assault. This particular one was known as Operation Torch.

Lt. Bernice Davis stood very still in line halfway back in the landing craft waiting her turn. Of the thirty-five soldiers tightly packed in the open boat, six were women nurses, but all looked the same as shades of fading moonlight bounced dully off their helmets. Bernice shivered in apprehension because she would be the first of the women to go into the water. Soldiers were exiting smoothly in threes, disregarding the confusion created by empty landing crafts randomly crashing into other boats. The noise of many engines thundered across the water and artillery fire overhead was aimed at the convoy they had just left. Her turn came. She took a deep breath, and the boat lurched and she stumbled off, her face plunging into the cold seawater. The strong arms of the two soldiers on either side of her pulled her up. Coughing, she gagged and spit salty water and bits of debris, oil blurring her eyes. Her wet backpack dragged her down as she pushed each leg forward against the heavy waves. Steadily, step after step against the pull of the waves, the soldiers pulled her onto the sandy beach. Falling to her knees, she froze in indecision, wondering for a moment what she was doing there. The shout came to crawl and take cover and crawl she did, feeling and hearing the grunting bodies around her. Dry vegetation scratched her face; rocks scraped her hands as she scrambled over sand and dirt trying with all her might to keep going and think of something nice. She closed her eyes and pictured herself in her mother's kitchen taking an apple pie out of the oven, the smell of cinnamon filling her nostrils as she snaked her way over the uneven ground. Banging against the musty smelling boards of a small shed, she lay quiet, grateful for its temporary security. Huddled against the boards, cold and wet, a sigh of relief escaped. She was glad that she was still alive.

When Bernice woke from a few hours of deep sleep she heard the whisper, "Move out. Keep the ocean on your left. No talking." Her eyes were gritty with sand, her lips caked with salt and her nose filled with motor fumes. Joining other anonymous shapes in the half dark, she trotted toward whatever destination had been chosen to establish a field hospital.

After all the soldiers had landed, the last landing craft nosed through the dense smoke screen carrying a huge truck marked with a blood red cross. It was the mobile operating hospital. Two lines of men pushed with muted grunts and groans, pulling the truck out of the water to safety and ignoring the distant explosions.

Like a ritual at each location, hospital tents were set up, used and then broken down and moved to follow the fighting. She had become close friends with the other nurses who shared her tent each with their own area of expertise. Leona, with red wiry hair and curves that defied the G.I. issue of men's uniforms they had to wear, Jean, tall, blond and handsome, married, but separated. Janet, petite and dependable, unmoved by bloody surgeries, Lucy, with the face of an angel who patted and hugged and had most of the patients half in love with her and Barbara, who had trained with Bernie at Ft. Lewis, was the comic, always smiling and joking, though Bernice knew underneath all the wisecracks was a deep insecurity. Barbara had made it clear she was getting out of the Army as soon as her years were up. Bernie as leader of the group drew up the schedule, rotating their eight hour shifts depending on the high or low load of incoming patients.

Supplies, medical equipment, even food, seemed never to quite catch up to them as they were moving. Water especially was scarce; sometimes there was none. Dust storms came up without warning, covering everything with hot, fine sand that plugged the nose and stung their eyes. The casualties became worse, caused by ground contact with the French forces. Many of those that were brought in were past help. Nurses shed tears by the gallon in private. Over the months, no discrimination could be made. A wounded patient was a wounded patient, whether he was a civilian, soldier, or prisoner of war. The German army attacked them in the mountain range, resulting in injuries to thousands of U.S. soldiers. After the first of the year, the joyful word came that the fighting was lessening.

Chapter 3

May, 1943 – Field Hospital

It was early May, 1943 in a field hospital tent in Tabarca. Bernice half woke in the dark to the sound of a truck rumbling to a stop.

Bernie heard a voice from the truck, saying, "This is it soldier. Can you make it on your own? Help him down, Joe."

The flap opened and a weary voice spoke, "Is this the hospital? I was sent to the hospital."

Bernice sat up on her cot and replied, "Yes, it is. Follow the flashlight beam to a cot. I will be right there." Slipping on her boots, she went to the man sitting on the edge of the cot.

"Where are you hurt, soldier? Can I take off your coat?"

"Take my coat. It's my leg, my left leg, shrapnel from a mine. They patched it up once. I don't know how long ago."

Bernice looked past at what remained of his dirt-caked trousers and the dark stained bandages, past his thin shoulders to the scared young man's dirty face. "Lie down on your right side and I will take care of it. I am going to cut your pants leg. You need a new pair anyway." Bernice cleaned the wounds, replacing the dressings with larger bandages and secured them tightly. "There, that didn't take long; let me get you settled. Are you hungry?"

"No, I couldn't eat anything, just thirsty."

Bernice searched through what was left of her food supply in the C-ration boxes for a juice can. She found a pair of striped pajama bottoms and handed them to the solder. "Here you go. I will put your boots and helmet right under your cot. Do you want some help?"

"I can do it. They died you know, both of them. Our truck blew up. We were just riding along and suddenly – no truck. We all got thrown out and started to walk. They stepped on a mine and died right there. My buddies…gone in a flash, so I just started running. So many men dead and I ran right over them. I fell and got up and ran some more. I can't go back! I just can't. I lost my friends." He was sobbing hoarsely, and then turned his face to the wall of the tent.

Bernice took a deep breath, as she dug in her pack for a sedative, one of the few remaining. She opened the juice can and handed it and the pill to the grieving soldier, smoothing the shirt over his shoulders and patting him. "Take this and get some sleep. Good night, see you in the morning." She walked through the tent, thankful that half the cots were empty and less wounded were coming in. Her flashlight danced over the sleeping men. She covered one with a blanket, picking up a dropped rosary and answered a whispered call for a urinal.

Sitting on her cot, she listened to the night sounds of men: coughing, snoring and moaning. Through the walls of the tent she heard the faint sound of a radio in the next tent playing "In the Mood".

A weak voice came from the newcomer in the first cot, "Bernie...Bern – is that you?"

"My name is Bernice, how did you know?"

"It's me, Gene. Remember – Eugene Harrington, from Ft. Lewis. We met at the USO there. I'm Sergeant Harrington now."

Bernice shook her head in surprise. Pouring a little water from her canteen on a cloth, she went to Gene and washed his face. "Well, there you are! We meet again. Who would have thought it would be here? Let me wash your hands too."

Gene flinched as she ran the cloth over his left hand. "I guess I must have fallen on something sharp."

Bernie directed the flashlight beam down so that it showed ragged cut across his palm. "I'll get something to put on that."

"I'm so glad to see you Bernie. You don't know how glad. I didn't think it could be so awful. My friends are dead, and I don't know where I am. I don't want to fight anymore. I can't do it. I want to go home."

"You are here with me in a hospital and you are going to get better. You will never forget your friends, but we all have to do our job as best we can. We all want to go home – and we will, sooner than you know. If you want to talk about the army, I know the right person. I talk to him myself sometimes. He's a doctor, not for your leg, but more for your head, someone to talk to about the war. A good night's sleep is what you need right now." She pulled the light blanket snug around his neck. She could see that his eyes were already closing. "That's it for you soldier, you need the sleep. Good night, Sergeant."

"Good night, Lieutenant."

As she passed by a new patient, shot by a sniper through the window of his truck, spoke in a trembling voice, "Can you sing, nurse?"

"I guess I can carry a tune. What's your name soldier?"

"Sandy. Everyone calls me Sandy. Do you know Amazing Grace?"

Bernice dragged a campstool next to him and began to sing quietly,

'Amazing Grace, how sweet the sound, that saved a wretch like me,"

He opened his mouth and in a true tenor voice sang, first hesitant, then stronger,

"I once was lost, but now I'm found." They sang together,

"Was blind, but now I see."

His voice grew stronger and wove around hers sweetly with a pure and startling timbre. He then sang alone and his voice filled the tent,

"Through many dangers, toils and snares,

I have already come; Tis grace hath brought me safe thus far,

And grace will lead me home."

A muffled sob was heard in the dark; a small voice from one of the beds whispered, "Amen."

Bernice patted the soldier's arm and thanked him. He groped under his pillow and handed her a letter. "Would you mail this for me in the morning? It's to my wife."

"Of course, now you close your eyes and go to sleep," she said, glad the darkness covered the wetness in her eyes.

Out of habit, Bernice woke before the sunrise, even before the morning nurse came. After gathering her pack together, she set it by the tent door and walked down the two aisles for one last check. Picking up the hand of the soldier that had sung with her, she could feel he was ice cold. After feeling for his pulse, she heaved a ragged sigh and folded hands over his chest. Opening the tent flap, she motioned to two soldiers outside. They came in quietly, picked up the soldier, cot and all.

She covered his face with his blanket and whispered. "Thank you for your song. Thank you for everything." Looking at the letter on her side table, she took it out and wrote on the back, 'I am a nurse in the field hospital where your husband is now. I want you to know he sang us a song last night. He has the most beautiful voice. He sang Amazing Grace and said it was a favorite. He wanted you to know he was thinking of you.' She signed it Lt. Bernice Davis, R.N.

A few days later Gene limped down the row of tents looking for the doctor Bernice had suggested. He found the tent with boxes and crates in front upended and waiting for the daily group of card players and read the small framed notice, Dr. Robert Clark, Mental Health. He stood motionless for a few minutes as trickles of perspiration from the unrelenting desert heat ran down his back wetting his shirt. He knocked lightly on the doorframe and was motioned in a by a tall, sandy haired solder.

Sit down son: I'm Dr. Clark. Lieutenant Davis sent you?"

"Yes sir, I need to talk to you."

"First tell me your name and rank and what division you belong to, then tell me about yourself. How and when did you get in the Army?" He scribbled as Gene answered.

"It seemed like the right thing to do when my brother got killed at Pearl. It made my mother unhappy but I was stupid and went ahead and joined.

"How were you wounded, Gene?"

Gene took a deep breath, closed his eyes and spoke in a soft voice, "Our truck hit a mine. It blew up and threw the three of us out the back. I went around the truck one way and my two buddies went around the other. One of them must have tripped on a mine and they just disappeared. I got shrapnel in my leg. They were just gone, sir, there was nothing left of them. Dick and Dave. We were together since we landed in November, wet and cold, snipers all around us. We stayed together across this godforsaken country in this crazy war. Now, it's just me. Just like that. I still can't believe it. I am tired and hurt. I hate the war. I hate everything about it, the noise, the dirt, the smell and the blood. I can't kill anybody. I can't sleep, I have nightmares. Why them and not me? I won't fight anymore. What's the point? Put that in your report. I want to go home. I will go AWOL if I have to."

"Who is at home waiting for you, Gene? Tell me about your family."

"Just my Mom and Dad. My older brother was in the Navy and died in Pearl Harbor. That's when I just had to quit college and join the service. My folks have a little grocery store in Portland, Oregon and live upstairs. We all lived upstairs. My brother and I grew up helping in the store. My Mom runs it now. My Dad got drunk when they heard the news about my brother, fell down the stairs and broke his leg. When they set his leg in the hospital, he just clammed up and hasn't been the same since. He can't work, or maybe he just won't. My Mom writes that she can't wait until I get out and come home to help her."

"Give me your brother's name and rank, son, and let me check into a few things. It will take a while, maybe a week. You just rest and get better. Come play cards or talk to me anytime."

After Gene left Dr. Clark wrote in red at the top of the page. 'Last son remaining. Wounded with battle fatigue. Suggest his return to Ft. Lewis, Washington.'

Chapter 4

LONDON, SHOPPING AND TEA

DECEMBER, 1943

Dozens of nurses met in Tunisia and boarded a
ship for the short trip to Sicily. The fighting ended in
the Sicilian Campaign in August in just over a month
and as day follows night, preparations were underway
for both the British and the Americans to invade Italy.
It was anticipated and did happen that Italy capitulated
almost instantly as troops and nurses landed in Salerno,
however, the Germans continued dropping bombs from
their fighter planes. The nurses went where they were
needed moving their hospital camps up the west coast
of Italy as winter approached. Fatigue, dysentery and
malaria took its toll on the women. Leona became ill
with malaria and had a short stay in the hospital.
Bernie's request for R and R for herself and her crew
seemed to be lost in paperwork. When the packet came
with the answer, it was not for rest and recreation but it

was a transfer to another post to set up a training school for nurses.

Bernice and her group of nurses left the fighting behind in Italy in November 1943 by ship, landing in Newport, England. They would teach, prepare and open a new hospital. Looking forward to a time of rest, they were excited to find their new home to be a castle outside of London.

Christmas was just then a week away and the three nurses decided to make the short train trip to London for shopping. Bernice, Leona and Jean dressed warmly and left early Saturday, exhilarated to be heading for the big city on the train. As they sipped warm tea in paper cups, they were silent, passing deep bomb craters, large grey stacks of rubble and sad remnants of homes. From the train station they took a bus to Piccadilly Square and found a small visitor kiosk with a few maps and brochures. They eagerly followed directions for several hours, ending up in front of Buckingham Palace, a corner of which was roped and sandbagged around a large bomb crater.

"Now I've seen everything," Leona said quietly.

Jean wagged her head, "Not so, we have to go to Harrods. We can't miss that. Come on we are wasting shopping time."

Two hours and many escalator rides later, Leona moaned, "I'm done shopping. There isn't much on the shelves anyway. My dogs are barking. Can we find something to eat?"

"Good idea. Let me ask someone. Bernice felt the scrutiny and met the eyes of a tall and tanned uniformed attendant as he opened the door for them. He was well over six feet tall with impossibly broad shoulders straining against rich green material of a uniform that must have been custom made. She made her way over to him, her heart thumping, and surprising warmth flooding her face. When her eyes met his sea green eyes, something, some recognition, some force, passed between them in an instant.

She stammered, "Can you direct us to a café, please?" High cheekbones and a narrow straight nose over a wide, generous mouth melded together into a striking face. A tiny jolt of pleasure caused her lips to curve spontaneously into a half smile and her eyes to open wide. With an easy smile, he pointed across the street to a small tearoom. His voice was deep and surprisingly rich with a British accent. He cupped her elbow lightly and turned her to face the street,

"There is a tea shop just there, Tibbits Tea Room, see the door? I think you would like their four o'clock tea and sandwiches. Try to sit next to the window so you can people watch."

An electric tingle began where his long fingers touched her arm. Bernice was unaware that she was holding her breath. His hand slid down her arm and squeezed hers. Her pulse racing, she hesitated, and then pulled her hand away. "Thank you, can you also suggest a nice place to eat dinner?"

"Yes, Lieutenant, I can. What time shall I pick you up?" He smiled broadly, his eyes twinkling.

Bernice chuckled nervously, "I would have to get rid of two soldiers."

"If we are going to have dinner, we should introduce ourselves. Trent Hamilton. I work here at Harrods part time."

"I'm Lt. Bernice Davis, and I am a soldier all the time." She turned as if in slow motion, and followed the other two nurses across the street into the café, taking seats in the window.

Jean bubbled and giggled, "He was handsome! He liked you Bernice, I could tell. He held your hand."

"Oh, he was just being polite. The uniform gets them every time." To change the subject, and cover her agitation, Bernice read out loud the stand-up card in the middle of the table aloud.

"If you are cold, tea will warm you. If you are heated, it will cool you.

If you are depressed, it will cheer you. If you are excited, it will calm you."

"That covers just about everything." Pots of tea arrived with three small grated carrot sandwiches, cut in quarters. Watching through the window, they could see the parade of limousines spill out their colorful contents of robes and turbaned shoppers. Three tall, haughty black women in long striped dresses that swept the ground, blared their colors of deep blue, magenta and gold, herded two young, noisy and enthusiastic boys in bright white pants and shirts. Bernice made no effort to hide her glances at the tall, attractive man in the glittering gold and green Harrods uniform. She watched as he hailed taxis, helped customers with packages and suitcases, gave directions, pointed, almost dancing on the balls of his feet. The outline of his body stretched taut in the form fitting materiel.

Jean noticed Leona staring at her half-eaten sandwich. "You are as white as a sheet!"

Tiny beads of sweat dotted Leona's forehead. She laid her head down on her arms saying, "I'm shivering. I feel like crap on a cracker. Either I am getting the flu or it's the malaria coming back."

Jean felt her friend's forehead, "You're cold? You feel like you are burning up. Take my muffler. Do you have any malaria pills with you?"

"Just a little back at the hotel, not enough to last until tomorrow."

Jean looked straight at Bernice, "Our shopping is over anyway. We have to take her back." Just then there was a break in the traffic and the tall doorman crossed the street.

Jean whispered, "Bernice, look who's coming, tall, dark and handsome."

"Hello ladies. How is everything?"

Jean was the first to stand, "The tea was fine, but our friend is sick and we need to leave now. If you can get us a taxi, we can get to our hotel and then the train. She can be in bed in an hour."

Trent spoke quickly, "Let me get a taxi for you, at that door right there." He put his silver whistle in his mouth, whistled all the way to the other side of the street, flagging a cab and opened its doors. The three nurses piled in, giving directions to their hotel. Standing on the sidewalk watching the cab drive away, he shook his head at the sight of a small palm pressed against the back window glass. Returning to his work in earnest, he began helping a group of women and children. He did not notice that the black vehicle had driven only halfway down the block, then slowed.

Jean looked at Bernice shrewdly, "Do you want to stay?"

After a moment, Bernice answered quietly, "He did ask me to dinner."

"Bernice, will you wake up tomorrow and wish you had? You would always wonder. I know I would. When was the last time you had a real date? We are in a war, Bernice. My motto is - live every day. We have already paid for the room; it would be a waste. Cabbie. Stop! Stop here. You can always shop some more. Stay Bernie… get away from it all for a weekend. We will be fine."

Bernie waited a moment to answer, "I think I want to stay. Most of the men I have met lately are in a hospital bed." Bernie gave Jean a big smack on the cheek, grabbed her purse and stepped to the curb. She stood very still as the taxicab made its way down the street. She did not hear the horns, the babble of pedestrians, or the screeching tires of a bus, just the beating of her heart. It was as if an invisible bubble had formed around the two of them. Unconsciously she leaned toward Trent, head down, waiting for him to notice her. Would he? What would he think? When he did turn toward her, he did a double take and lost his grip on a briefcase. Throwing the case carelessly in a trunk, he walked to her, eyes fastened on hers. Placing both hands on her shoulders, he squeezed hard, saying,

"So Lieutenant; how about that dinner? I am through with work. It will take about five minutes for me to get into my street clothes."

Chapter 5

DINNER AND A PICNIC

A small blue light was all that directed them, first down a side street, and then an alley. Trent opened the unmarked door to a small café that gave off tantalizing aromas of garlic and tomato sauce. Dinner was Italian. Noise of dishes clattering and the buzz of conversation rose across the red checkered tablecloths. A man who was obviously the owner, and had a fair sized paunch under a huge handlebar mustache, threw his arms around Trent roaring,

"Too long I have not seen you! Come this way...a very special table for you and your soldier lady." Leading them to a tiny alcove at the side of the restaurant, he clapped his hands. "Waiter...setups please, and a bottle of wine, from me to you. Coming are menus."

"We don't need menus, Guido, just bring us soup, bread and spaghetti, and don't hurry."

The Chianti came first, then minestrone with dots of grated cheese, then warm bread with chunks of garlic, and finally huge piles of spaghetti in deep bowls, with small bits of meat and red sauce, lots of fragrant red sauce. They talked all through the meal and dawdled over coffee with a splash of rum. Trent pulled her to him and kissed the point of her nose.

Bernice moved away and said, "I think we should talk a little first."

Trent told his story. "My father was going to school here and worked part time in the tea shop where you ate. My mother worked in the Dutch Embassy here in London. They met at the teashop and fell in love, and later got married at her Embassy. There was trouble brewing just before the war and my father was called home to India. My mother wasn't ready to go then, so he promised to send for her. She didn't know she was pregnant with me. The tradition in his family was that children were promised to each other when very small, and he was forced to follow that tradition and marry his family's choice. So he never sent for Mum. He wrote her when his first daughter was born and she wrote back and told him he also had a son. The owners of the teashop befriended her and asked her to work for them so she raised me all alone. When I was born they let her bring me to work, so I really grew up in the teashop. Mrs. Tibbits owns the teashop and the house where I live. We lived in a loft room but when I got bigger we moved downstairs and Mrs. Tibbits moved upstairs.

She was alone by that time, but after the Blitz, she sold the teashop and went to Northern Scotland to be with her daughter. She just said 'Goodbye; take care of the house.' I made a deal with my father after my Mum died last year and he is paying for my college. I am almost finished. I am studying business economics and marketing. I just work shifts at Harrods between classes. The sad part is that my Mum was a volunteer ambulance driver; and she was killed during the London Blitz. I've talked enough…I want to hear more about you."

Bernice took his hands in hers, "I am so sorry about your mother. This is a horrible war and we are not through it yet. I was just a farm girl, fourth out of seven kids, born on my parents' hundred acres in Washington State. My mother just got tired of hard work and having children and died when I was in high school. I did most of the cooking after that. My sister Rose wanted to go to school to be a nurse but my father was very strict. He said it was not a fit profession for an unmarried woman. At about that time, my father married again, a gal almost young enough to be his daughter. Some of the other kids weren't too happy about that. Rose secretly packed her bags and snuck in to my room to tell me to get out of there too. 'One of these days Bernice, get a good job and see other places.' The very next week when I was in town doing our shopping, I passed by a poster that said 'Uncle Sam Wants You for the U.S. Army.' I thought about that poster all the time when I was doing my shopping. So I put everything in the car and went back. His finger was pointing right at me! I just figured that it was what Rose meant. I was almost twenty five and my father was calling me an old maid. I walked in to the Recruiting office and signed up for the Army. That was July of 1940. I started nurses' training in Ft. Lewis and my first real post was Northern Africa. It was exciting to me. I have to say I love my job, helping people get well. Sometimes it's sad, but most of the time it's good, meeting people. The nurses have become just like a big family."

Bernice groaned, "I could end up in the hospital if I don't stop eating. This is just about as far from army rations as you can get. No more wine. I am full, happy and a little dizzy."

His fingers wrapped around the fabric of her sleeves, then slid up her arm to trace the curve of her chin. "I like the happy part. I'll get a cab and take you home. Where is your room?"

"At the Cumberland; I have a card in my purse." The Cumberland was a short distance across from the Marble Arch. She shivered and Trent put his arm around her. Bernice luxuriated in the warmth of the cab and his possessiveness as he tucked her under his shoulder. They were in a small, secure realm of their own. Outside, the wind was trying to get in; an occasional searchlight flashed brightly through the fog. She was sleepy and the lulling warmth of the wine had made her a little tipsy. Enveloped by the rich scent of sandalwood and calmed by the rhythmic pounding of the tires, her eyes closed. After stopping in front of the hotel, Trent paid the cabbie and Bernice whispered nervously,

"I guess this is where the gal asks if the guy wants a nightcap."

He gathered her in his arms, pressing her against him, "This is where the guy answers, yes."

As she fumbled with the key in the door, Trent turned her to him and said solemnly, "I want you to know, I really want to kiss you."

"I want it too; can you open this damn door?"

Trent kicked the door shut behind him and reached for Bernice. Her mouth was open before his arms circled her; his mouth covered hers fully and intimately. His lips felt warm and full. She could taste the richness of rum and coffee. After kissing her face and neck, he held her away from him, looking into her eyes. "I wanted to kiss you in front of Harrods. I wanted to kiss you in the teashop. Sky blue eyes, do we have something going on here?"

Bernice murmured "I think so. Can you hear my heart pounding? If you weren't holding me I think I would fall." Moonlight winked around the blackout shades, guiding Trent a few steps toward the bed with her in his arms.

"Sit on my lap so I can hold all of you. I have a confession. I sent you to the teashop so I could watch you. I wanted…I just felt drawn to you." He was talking between soft kisses. "Are we wrinkling your uniform?"

His legs felt strong beneath her, and warmth spread between them. Bernice sighed, "I should hang it up, but I don't want to move."

Trent began to unbutton her jacket, then her blouse. "I'll help you." He kissed her neck while his fingers lightly explored her breasts, whispering. "I don't do this, you know."

She tipped her head back, "What do you mean, you don't 'do this'?"

"I mean I don't pick up women, take them to dinner and then to a hotel room."

Bernice laid her head on his shoulder, breathing into his neck, "Then why me?"

His tongue followed his fingers down the curve of her breast, "I don't know; your blue eyes, that crazy curly hair, your sweet mouth. I just knew I had to see you again." She held up her arms to help him as he slipped off her blouse and undershirt. Her small, petite body was pale and almost translucent in the moonlight. As their kisses became deeper and more demanding, she arched her back, needles of sensation flooding her body. She whispered, "Surely, I am not the first women you have ever wanted."

"I had a girlfriend on and off last year, a senior from Sweden. After her graduation, her father came and took her home, out of harm's way" As he covered her body with his, she chuckled deep in her throat.

"Is something funny?"

Sliding her hands up to his face, "Oh, No, Most men I meet are patients, sick and wounded. My first beau was a fumbling farmer, who knew his something went into my something; that's about all he knew. My next was a frightened solder. He was lonely; I was lonely. He tried but ended up crying in my arms. I've had other men friends, but none of them clicked. I guess you can blame that on the war. War makes a person realize that you need to live each day. Some moments will never come again. Your skin feels like silk. I can't stop touching you." His skin was smooth and warm and his body large over her. She welcomed the weight of him. She moved beneath him, opening her legs to his touch. His fingers traced up and down her side and between her thighs, "Cotton panties make me crazy. Take these off." He rose quickly and undressed, lying naked on his side next to her whispering, "You are exquisite. I want to make this the most beautiful, special night for you. I want to kiss you and touch you. Everything we do, I want you to remember. Then I want to go to sleep with you."

He was true to his word and later unbidden tears formed in her eyes, running down the side of her face onto the pillow. One small quiet sob turned into several bigger sobs until she was crying steadily, still held within his arms. Trent pulled back, "have I hurt you?'

Bernice took a deep breath, "No, don't think that. Why…why didn't I know about this? Why hasn't anyone told me? I'm not hurt. It's just so…emotional. It's as if something huge just broke in me, the most amazing incredible explosion, and then wave after wave of pleasure. I have been missing this. I didn't know what a climax was. Each time you moved, you seemed to go deeper inside me and touch a place I never even knew about. I am fine. Sorry about the crying."

Trent pulled the blankets and comforter around them, nestling close to her, "Let me hold you."

Trent was out of the shower and dressing when Bernice woke. After crossing to the bed, he took her hands and kissed them. "I didn't think to tell you I have to work half a day today. I wish I didn't, but I do. This is a busy season at Harrods. What do you think about staying with me tonight at my flat? Check out of here and meet me at the tearoom for lunch."

The idea excited her. At that point, she would have promised him anything. She reached out to him, a big smile on her face, "I'll be there."

When the cabbie pulled up in front of Tibbits Tearoom, Trent was standing in the doorway with a picnic basket. As their eyes met, her heart began to race, the memory of last night still vivid in her head.

He climbed into the cab saying, "I had them make up some sandwiches and things for a picnic. We can go somewhere quiet and have lunch". He gave an address to the cabbie, and then kissed her slowly, opening her lips with his tongue. His hand moved under her skirt to the soft skin of her inner thigh. Startled at the unexpected flash of desire, a moan started in her throat,

"No, no. Not in the cab."

Trent broke from their embrace, leaning forward to the driver redirecting him to a different address, and then whispered in her ear,

"We'll have our picnic at my place."

The cab pulled up to a corner behind another cab. "My house is the second one back. They made this an official cab stand when my mother had emergency calls to drive the ambulance." Unlocking the wide oak door at the top of the stairs, he set the basket inside, slammed the door shut and, with his body, pushed Bernice against the wall. Lifting her under the arms, knocking off the ear piece of the wall phone, he adjusted her body to his pressing himself between her thighs. He put her legs around his waist and rocked back and forth into her. "I can't wait, I want you right here, on the floor, on the steps. Sit on the landing." She sprawled back on the hard wood. He spread her legs, one foot kicking over the picnic basket.

Bernie tried to sit up, "The phone…the basket." In a thick voice, he growled, "Later." His arms lifted her and carried her up the stairwell.

His bed was just a mattress on the floor, made neatly with plump pillows and a thick down coverlet. Scattering their clothing, they tumbled together; his urgency spread to her and when he pushed himself into her, the feeling was intense. They moved together in a ferocious rhythm until her body stiffened, moaning, she dug her fingers into his back. A moment later he collapsed onto her with a shout.

By her side, breathing hard, he took her hand and kissed it saying, "I am sorry if I was rough but it just came over me. Let's have our picnic and I'll be slower next time.'

Bernice didn't know whether to pretend to close her eyes or stare fully at the sight of his broad honey-brown back and firm buttocks as he walked down the stairs naked. Coming back up, the basket obscured some of his body, but not enough to keep her from enjoying the frontal view.

"Aren't you worried about the people who live downstairs? They could open the door anytime. Has anyone ever told you that you are a beautiful man?"

Sitting the basket on the kitchenette table, he laughed, "Not likely. No one lives downstairs now. It was mine and Mum's before she died. After that, I moved up here. It's just easier to keep up. Everything down there is just as she left it. I'll get some robes and see what we can get on the shortwave." They devoured the sandwiches, two tiny salads, and an orange, with a bottle of cider, while the short wave radio was playing music.

Bernice looked up at Trent saying, "What is that gorgeous song?"

Trent smiled, "I guess that's our song. It's 'Clair de Lune, one of my favorites, great music for lovers."
Bernice brushed crumbs from her lap, saying "I think I'll freshen up. May I take a shower?"

"You take a shower and I'll make us a cuppa tea."

"But you don't have a kitchen."

He walked to the closet doors and opened them wide to show a tiny kitchen, small sink, hotplate, toaster and teapot, "Just big enough for me."

Bernice luxuriated in the needles of spray, washing her hair and body with a sliver of his Sandalwood soap. Leaning her forehead against the shower wall, her face flushed as she thought about Trent and their bodies together. After pulling a terry robe around her, she took the tea from him. Warming her hands on the tea mug, a hint of a smile crossed her face when she saw four little cookies on small plate edged in gold.

"My turn." Trent disappeared in the bathroom. The shortwave crackled and faded in and out. As Bernice fiddled with the knobs, the nasal voice of a newscaster chattered, and then a jazz pianist poured out melodic notes. She noticed a thin pale blue paper under the radio. Lifting the radio, she could see the bottom words on the paper which was signed 'Your Father, Dr. Omar Sanjay.' Lifting the radio further, she read, and then read it again.

'Dear Trent,

I am writing you as a Father would to his son, his only son, with great satisfaction in your accomplishments. Enclosed is a cheque for the remainder of your school year and graduation, and a cheque for you to welcome the bride I am sending you. She is of good family and the oldest of four girls. She is a teacher at the same school as your oldest sister. I am a good friend of her father and he has agreed to allow her to come to you. Be assured she is not fat or ugly, but she is tall. Her name is Amalli. She will be flying into Staunton airport with a companion on a charter plane. I have told her you would be there to meet her. You should marry within a few days. My best wishes for your future. Until I see you again, I remain Your Father, Dr. Omar Sanjay. '

A cold chill started in her chest and spread until she could not move. Her numb fingers dropped the letter. She folded the paper, fumbling, then folded it again, slipping it deep under the radio, wondering why he didn't tell her…but then why would he? How could he be with me and get married next week? But he is not mine…and I am not his. He is hers. This is his debt to his father. He had a life before me and has his own life now. So do I. I have to get out of here. I need to leave. I have to think of something to say.

Automatically, she began picking up her clothes avoiding the sight of the bed. Clenching her fists, she walked over to the rumpled bed and straightened the comforter and pillows turning her head to avoid the deep sweet smell of sex clinging to the sheets. Dressed, with tea mug in hand, she stood on tiptoe at the dormer window, relieved to see a cab parked at the corner. Trent came from the bathroom pulling on his robe. "You are dressed! I thought we would take a little sleep together."

Bernice drank the cold tea and cleared her throat, "Your war correspondent, Edward R. Murrow just announced Fats Waller has died, you know, the piano player. I think I should get back. We have been told not to be on the train after dark."

Trent put his arms around her, "I was hoping you would stay the night."

"I wish I could but I have to go. I have a class in the morning. I see a cab there and I don't want to miss it. It's starting to rain." She handed him her teacup and as he turned to put it down, she slipped her shoulder bag over her shoulder, grabbed her overcoat and hurried to the stairs.

As she walked down the stairs, he was close behind, hands on her shoulders,

"I have to say I'm disappointed, really disappointed. It feels like you have only been here a few minutes, a handful of minutes. Are you sure you can't stay the night and go in the morning?" She didn't answer. "Let me go with you to the station at least."

"No, this is best. I really have to go. You know I have to go. We get up very early for a meeting. Don't come out. One goodbye is enough. Every time I hear Claire de Lune, I will think of you. Even the most beautiful day has to end. Thank you for it. Don't come outside. It's raining." Arms around his neck, she held him tight for a moment as he kissed her closed lips. Pulling away from him she ran to the cab and didn't look back.

"So long Trent."

"Keep safe, soldier."

Chapter 6

THE JOB SEARCH

LONG BEACH, CALIFORNIA – April – 1967

The friendship of Bernice and Barbara Barnes began when they met at Ft. Lewis finishing their nurses training while in the Army. They roomed together, studied together and were both happy and proud to graduate together and receive their honorary second lieutenant bars on one shoulder and the caduceus on the other. It was luck that they came together in Africa. They then worked together through those months in Africa and on up into Italy. Bernice realized early in those months of the war, that Barbara couldn't wait to get out of the army. Barbara's only reason for enlisting was to have a job and earn a living.

Bernice, however, thoroughly enjoyed her work and when she finally made the decision to retire after twenty six years at the rank of major, she packed up all the letters received from Barbara over the years, reading the last one again.

Barbara had married and had become Mrs. Walter Stern shortly after leaving the service. They had purchased a duplex in Long Beach, California where their son Jack was born. Walter had died unexpectedly when Jack was in the eighth grade. Barbara had repeated her appeal in her last letter which was for Bernice to come to Long Beach and rent the other side of the duplex and Bernice had decided that it would be a good idea. So they had become neighbors as well as friends. A year went by and she had settled in.

Bernice tossed and turned looking for a favorite position, but sleep wouldn't come. She didn't know why she was so restless. She liked living next to her good friend. Her retirement checks came in every month; her years in the Army had been a good job for her and she no longer needed to work. So why did she feel like she wanted to do something? She tried telling herself she would think about it in the morning.

Morning came and Bernice made coffee and consulted the newspaper classifieds for jobs... accountants, bank employees, cashiers, food service, garbage men, hotel clerks and maids, hospital volunteers, morticians, mother's helpers for four children, night watchman, pilot, real estate salesmen, truck driver - must have own truck. Nothing there for her. She didn't want to volunteer; she'd done her share of that in hospitals. She found two employment companies that said they had jobs waiting.

Bernice dressed carefully in her best navy blue suit and pearl earrings. She put her head down, brushed her salt and pepper curls vigorously, and stood up patting the sides of her hair and took the bus downtown. Standing in front of the first address, she could not see through the soap swirled over the windows, but she could see the sign that said closed for remodeling. One down, one to go. The second address was on the 11th floor of a twelve story building just off Ocean Avenue. The frosted door glass declared 'Acme Employment.' In the office she took a seat along with several other women, all younger.

The receptionist handed her a clipboard. "Please fill out this appointment interview, with your name, address and work history, It will help us know more about you." Bernice filled it in quickly, handing it back to the surprised secretary.

She scanned it, "Hmmm. You are done first. Take this and go in."

The smartly dressed woman behind the desk got up and extended her hand. "My name is Alma. Thank you for coming. I hope we can help you. Let me explain how this works. The employer pays me something in advance, and if you stay three months on the job, you pay me two weeks of your salary. Let us see what I have in my card file for someone your age. Bank elevator operator? Food Server at Mannings? Hotel Help? Nanny? Housemother for a retarded adult home? Cook companion for a single man? Manager of a senior center? Stop me when you want to talk about one of them."

Bernice shook her head and sighed, "None of those are what I am looking for. I really don't know what I am looking for. What about the one that wants a cook-companion? I am a good cook."

Alma smiled and raised her eyebrows, "Good, this is an interview in North Long Beach. It just says 'must drive, must cook, especially apple pie and chicken and dumplings, and must be free to travel.' No age is mentioned. I can phone and make the appointment for you. Here is the address."

After another bus ride, an attractive gray-haired woman answered the door of the bright yellow house on Lemon Street. They introduced themselves and sat at the maple dining room table where tea was already set up and waiting. They had tea and talked for a while. Bernie explained her background expressing that she just wanted to do something more in her life.

"Bernice, I like you very much, but I must tell you that the job is not with me, but with my brother. He is laid up with gout right now, and I am looking over the people who apply. I am ready to tell him that I think you are the one, but after you hear the whole story, you have to decide. The job is not here. In fact, you would be flying to Mexico to live and work in a beautiful new home he has built. It is on a hill overlooking a lake; I have pictures, let me show you." They spent a companionable hour finishing their tea and a whole plate of peanut butter cookies. Bernice marveled at the photo of the white domed creation built by what might be her new employer, Harlan Walters.

"This is the little house for you, in the back yard. They call it a casita. Here is a picture of us when we were little and here is one of him now with his son and daughter in law. They live in Modesto. They call Harlan 'The Colonel' because he owns a big chicken ranch there. But he wants to retire and give the farm over to his son, who is a police officer. Think about this now, dear. This is a big decision and a long way for you to move. There is just one more thing. He would like you to make dinner for me, and if that goes well, I will tell him to send you an airplane ticket. If you don't like the job, he will send you back."

Bernice sat quietly for a few minutes, her mind racing. She looked one more time at the picture of the man with white hair. Smiling broadly, she answered, "I don't know how I can lose. The worst that can happen is that I meet some new people and have a vacation. I could like it there. I have traveled to many countries but never to Mexico. It does sound grand. When would you like to have dinner?"

Chapter 7

SUNDAY BRUNCH – THE NEXT HOUR'

LAKE CHAPALA – 1980

As Bernie's story unfolded, a second pitcher of margaritas quietly appeared. Bernie was finishing her special starter, which was a soup bowl half filled with chunky fresh fruit to which she had added generous blobs of delicious creamy yogurt and topped with granola bits.

With her mouth full, Bernie exclaimed, "The best damn yogurt and cheese I've ever tasted is made right here in Mexico."

Just then Juana, the owner of the restaurant, tall and stately, brought over two trays of sliced vegetables, put them in the center of the table and took the last empty seat, saying,

"Hello ladies, may I join you for lunch? This is the best part of my Sunday, watching everyone serve themselves"

Bernie introduced Juana as a longtime friend to Linda, and the owner of El Gallo Poco, explaining she and Maigret had found Juana and the restaurant about twelve years ago when they first arrived and added, "This place is our second home."

Juana and Maigret met at the steaming chocolate pot and topped their fragrant brew with freshly made whipped cream. Bernie watched Linda Lou eat sparingly at first, amazed by the dazzling array of foods. Linda walked up and down the counter, lifting the lid of each metal pan, standing open mouthed in front of luscious fruits and berries in rich colors, sliced cheese, diced cheese, soft cheese, crumbly anejo cheese, yogurt, sour cream, whipped cream and cold meat platters with many different meats. Luscious pink shrimp on a bed of ice and lemon slices, scrambled eggs, eggs Benedict, hard boiled eggs, red potatoes with onions, chilaquiles, empanadas, thick bacon and steaming sausages. There was sliced ham, roast chicken, huge mushrooms, soup, paella and a corner set up for waffles and omelets made to your order.

Linda Lou pointed, "What is that, and what is this, the thin meat? What is this fruit - the one that is shaped like a star? I love fruit, but I don't eat much meat. I don't know what to choose."

Bernie came up next to Linda, "Let me help you. From the looks of you, you need to eat more of this good stuff. Bernie filled Linda's plate with yogurt on top of fresh fruit, cubes of cheese, roast chicken, two huge shrimp and a crusty roll.

Maigret covered her plate with fresh fruit, yogurt, sliced ham and a flaky sugar covered breadstick to dip in her chocolate, then ordered a mushroom omelet from Carmen, the cook, who was behind the waffle and omelet corner.

Linda finished half her plate and all of her glass of mango juice and poured the tall glass full from the margarita pitcher. "Who wants a little glash when you can save time and have a big one, I mean glass. What is this thick stew with the shrimp and all those other things?"

Juana answered with pride, "My grandmother taught me how to make that, it's called paella. It's a special Spanish dish. I think you will like it."

Bernie stood looking at the cakes longingly. "Which ones did you bring?"

Maigret pointed to the two cakes she had brought. One was a rich looking chocolate and walnut cake with creamy tan frosting, covered with shavings of chocolate curls. The other was a white chocolate truffle cake with whipped cream filling, decorated with dollops of yellow icing.   Linda spoke to Maigret, "Where are you from Maigret? How did you pick this place?"

"Bernice and I were neighbors and good friends in Long Beach. She came to my wedding. When she came down here for her job, I just tagged along when my son was just a baby. I fell in love with everything and never looked back. My name is really Margaret but here my friends call me Maigret. People say sometimes things happen for the best and when I look back I think I was meant to be here. Let me tell you how I met Bernice."

Chapter 8

MARGARET - 1966

LONG BEACH, CALIFORNIA

It was 5:05 p.m. A tall blond was waiting for her best friend, Margaret, outside the elevators in the building where they both worked, and she was tapping her foot impatiently. Spring and Margaret both came from the cold winters of Montana to live and work in sunny California. When her friend appeared, Spring grabbed her arm and said,

"Come on Margaret, its Friday night and its hot. Let's do something. Let's walk the Pike and I'll buy you a hot dog and a coke. "

Dodging the increasing crowd of amusement seekers and giggling about the sailors, Margaret watched with wide eyes as Spring stepped between the Arcade and a Pop the Balloon stand. She shook her head as Spring pulled her bra straps down over each arm and unsnapped it in the back. Yanking the lacy lingerie out over the front of her blouse, she stuffed it in her purse, tightening the blouse into her skirt band.

"I'm going to give those sailor boys something to look at," said Spring.

Margaret rolled her eyes and hissed, "I can see everything!'

"Good, then so can they."

Two sailors dogged the steps of the girls zigzagging their way through the crowded rows of games and amusement trailers.

"Keep up J.R., we're losing them. I want the blond," urged the taller sailor. The other sailor replied,

"Max, you will screw anything that walks."

"Not so my friend, you are only half right, but if it is female, it is definitely under consideration."

J.R's face flashed a big smile, "Fine with me, the other one is just my size, prettier too."

Max purposely stepped on the back of Spring's heel and she stumbled and turned, her breasts loose and bouncing. Staring at the pink points through the thin material and the swell of white skin, he groaned,

"I think I'm in love. Where are you going, pretty lady?"

Spring turned facing the young men, standing straight and then arched her back, "We're going to get a corn dog and because you are so rude, you can buy. There's a place we go to just up ahead.

Max stepped closer, smiling and looking down "You have to tell me your name first."

"I'm Spring Russell, and this is my friend, Margaret."

Six feet of Max pointed to five foot two J.R. "I'm Max and this is my buddy, Jack, but J.R. for short."

Jack fell in step with Margaret and looked at her admiringly, "You are really pretty, ya know. Lucky me. Do you want a corn dog? I'll buy you one, or popcorn?'

Looking straight ahead, Margaret tried not to smile, "Mm, popcorn would be nice."

Spring ordered a corn dog with double mustard and Max paid. She walked away from the stand, licking the bright yellow mustard dripping down the stick. Her small white teeth bit carefully into the dough from the top down. Out of the corner of her eye she could see that Max could not take his eyes off her tongue licking the dripping mustard.

Groaning, Max put his hands over his face, "You're killing me. I can't look. God, I need a beer. J.R., how about we all get a beer? Let's mosey on up to the Sub Room."

Margaret wrinkled her nose, "I'm not going in there, it smells. It smells just walking by. I think the Ferris wheel would be more fun."

Jack touched her arm and said pleadingly, "Just five minutes. If you don't want a beer, have a Coke. There's a neat aquarium with miniature submarines and tropical fish. You might like it."

Jack's reddish crew cut and freckles were the perfect setting for his light blue eyes. Walking with his hands jammed in the front pockets of his bright white uniform, he kept sneaking admiring peeks at Margaret. Jack and Margaret dropped behind the two in front, listening to them banter back and forth. Max, a head taller than his friend, was a big, muscular man, with dark wavy hair, a large smiling, open face, huge brown eyes and a mouthful of large, very white teeth.

Max kept up the teasing, "Oh baby, I think you were in my dreams last night. If I follow you home, will you keep me? Can I have your phone number; I've lost mine." He bumped his arm into Spring's arm trying to look down her blouse. The four entered the smoky tavern and as Max walked by the bar, he ordered,

"Draw two, and make mine a boilermaker." He steered Spring to the last booth, stepping aside so she would sit in the back corner. The seats were well used benches with high backs, giving ample privacy for customers. Max laid his arm around Spring's shoulder, hugging her to him, pushing her breasts up and partly out and he sighed softly. When Jack reached the booth, Max was pulling down her blouse, exposing an expanse of white skin.

"Jeez, Max, get a room." Jack took Margaret by the shoulders, turning her towards the bar and the green-blue fluorescent aquarium.

"They are smooching a little so let's look at the fish. See the treasure chest? It has real money in it."

After Margaret finished her Coke, she called to Spring, "I'm ready to go, let's go." Spring answered back faintly from inside the booth, "You go on Margaret – we're going to go dancing at the Starbrite Room. I won't be late."

Margaret walked out before Jack into the first twinkling lights of dusk. Margaret let him hold her hand all the way to the bus stop on Pine Boulevard,

"I like holding your hand." It didn't make the front of his pants tighten like the sight of a bare breast, but he liked touching her; he liked it a lot. Jack took a deep breath and said, "Can I call you? Or would you meet me next Sunday? We could go to a movie."

"Oh, I don't know. I was planning to bake gingerbread. I usually bake on Sundays."

"Aw, come on. Let's go on the Ferris Wheel then. You can't be doing anything as fun as that. We'll get popcorn and everything."

Margaret looked up at the neon signs flaring along the streets and smiled, "I'd like that. What time? Say eleven, or noon?" She turned as she boarded the bus. "What does J.R. stand for anyway?"

"It's John Robert, John Robert Stern – but everyone calls me Jack, or sometimes J.R."

"Jack." Margaret repeated the name. "I like it. See you right here next Sunday, Jack." Looking back, she could see him waving for several blocks. She folded her arms on the cold metal bar of the seat in front of her, putting her head down and closing her eyes. She could smell his scent on her, Ivory Soap and Old Spice. He is kind of cute, she thought. Maybe I could like him.

J.R. coaxed Margaret, "Open your eyes Margaret and look how far you can see. There, two chairs down, see those three swabbies. One lost his hat, poor bugger."

Margaret's eyes opened slowly and her view swept across the fortune teller booth, the tops of colorful tents and flags and the strip of arcades along the boardwalk. The chant of the barkers, chattering people along with the bright merry-go-round music floated up to her ears. The aromatic smell of popcorn filled her nose.

Margaret gritted her teeth and gripped the steel security bar of the silver blue Ferris wheel with white knuckled intensity. It hadn't seemed so terrifying from the ground. "Oh, this is so cool...but I can't look down."

"Then just close your eyes and listen to the fat lady laughing." Margaret closed her eyes and Jack leaned over and kissed her full on the mouth.

Her eyes flew open, "You tricked me! You are awful."

"It was worth it and I'm going to do it again."

"Not while we are up here, you're not! Look at my hands next to yours. You have small hands for a man."

"Small hands help with my job. I am in communication, ya know. I type all day, ship to shore, ship to ship, messages and information. I can type pretty fast."

"What kind of messages?"

"I can't say. I have security clearance for Navy stuff." Just then the Ferris wheel gave a series of jumps and starts, and then continued jerkily to the ground. Margaret cried out with a mewing sound. Jack put his arm around her. "Hey I'm here: I've got you. See that cotton candy stand...let's head for that." On the ground and happy that the hurtling ride was over, they quickly had pink cotton candy all over their hands and faces. Jack peered closely at Margaret's face.

"You have cotton candy on your lip; let me get it off." He bent close, licked her lip and quickly put his tongue in her mouth, kissing her soundly. "Mm, that was sweet. Come on, let's play some games and win a prize. What do you want to play? Ring toss? I think they are crooked. Pop the balloon? That's too easy. There...that one, the water rifles where you shoot the ducks. We'll both shoot." Jack won easily; his prize was a striped long-legged sock monkey. "Now, if you were really my girl, I would give this to you." he teased. "Or I could sell it to you for a kiss." Margaret got the monkey and more kisses there, and at the corner waiting for the bus.

Jack and Margaret dated all summer every day he had off and Margaret was happy to see him and to be with him. They took the bus to the beach with their swim suits several times, playing in the sand and water and eating fish and chips on newspaper from a beach front stand.

Jack loved the movies and they would sit in the dark, holding hands at first, but always ending with enthusiastic kisses. They would eat pizza at the Silver Dollar Pizza where the owners knew them by name. One Sunday, they went to visit Jack's home where he lived with his mother, but on that day Jack knew his mother was not going to be there. As Jack had hoped, after a rush of ardent kissing and stroking, he guided Margaret into his basement bedroom, evidence of his high school events on every wall. They undressed and got under the covers. Embarrassed, Margaret turned her back to him. Jack put his arms around her, lightly smoothing her breasts. Neither very aggressive, they just cuddled naked under the blankets until suddenly Jack groaned and said, "Aw damn, now it's too late."

They were both quiet for a long time. Jack asked, "Do you like me Margaret, really like me? I want us to be together. I was thinking we could get married, and then we would really have time. We could stay at Mother's for a while until we get our own place. What do you think?"

Margaret was dressing in a hurry, avoiding the eyes of the fresh faced student in the 8 x 10 picture on the dresser. A jumble of thoughts flooded her head, including the cramped quarters and lumpy couch she slept on at Spring and Mary Ann's small rental. The three had been best friends all through Havre High

School; those two had left the snow of Montana for the warm California weather, urging Margaret to come visit them. Three women and one bathroom were fine for visiting, but not forever. She really liked Jack, but did she love him? She liked to be with him, but was that love? Did she want to get married? "Get dressed Jack. Your mother could come home any minute. I'm not sure if we should get married." They dressed quickly and were sitting silently on the front porch when Mrs. Stern drove into the driveway.

Mrs. Stern smiled broadly as she walked past the couple to open the door, "You kids are so cute. You could go in, you know."

"Guess what Mom; we've been talking about getting married."

Blushing red, and uncomfortable, Margaret looked away and did not speak.

Margaret White married Third Class Petty Officer John Robert Stern two weeks later on a hot August afternoon in the downtown Long Beach Baptist Church. Spring and Max were their witnesses. Jack's mother brought her good friend and neighbor, Bernice Davis. Barbara Stern's eyes were bright with tears. Borrowing his mother's car, Jack drove them to the Edgewater Hotel, looking forward eagerly to their two nights of honeymoon. The small hotel orchestra finally called last dance.

The newlyweds looked into each other's eyes and Jack said, 'Let's go home Mrs. Stern." When they opened the door to their hotel room they could see a bright, cellophane wrapped fruit and cheese basket on their table, compliments of the hotel.

"Oh, Jack, isn't this wonderful? I really didn't get to eat much today. Can we have a little something, cheese and crackers? Let me get out of this dress. I'll put on my new nightgown and we can just sit for a few minutes - together." Jack took off his shoes and opened the basket pulling out the cracker packages and the cheese ball, lining everything up in a row.

"Come out, Mrs. Stern. I have a little snack for you."

Margaret slipped her leg around the bathroom door half showing a lacy piece of lingerie.

"Mrs. Stern, are you flirting with me?"

Margaret ran to him laughing, giving him a big hug. "Sit down Jack. Let me sit on your lap and we can have some of this basket," which they did, between kisses.

This time Jack was slow, touching her body in tender wonder and marveled that she was his wife. It was three in the morning when Jack's eyes closed, then Margaret's', their breath mingling on the crisp hotel sheets. They were happy and content with each other.

MARGARET

Chapter 9

MARGARET WAITS

LONG BEACH, CALIFORNIA –MAY, 1967

Margaret had a cold. She had hoped it would be over in a few days, but it was one of those nasty, runny nose, coughing, feels like an elephant stepped on your chest colds. It hung on for almost two weeks, her cough getting worse in the last few days. Her mother in law was getting worried about her coughing every few minutes.

"Margaret, you should go to the doctor about that cough. The baby is due in two weeks and it can't be good to shake him up like that."

Margaret hated the Navy Hospital on the base, including her doctor. Busy and overworked, he had no real time to spend with each patient. "Last week when I was there, he gave me a jar of mentholatum, cherry cough syrup and cough drops. He just told me to take aspirin and drink lots of juice, but none of it helped." Her face was white and pinched as she half sat, half lay on the couch, wiping her nose.

Her mother in law adjusted the pillow behind Margaret. "I'm going to make you some Campbell's chicken noodle soup - that should taste good - and some toast. Then I am going to call MY doctor, at least I can talk to her." Dr. McBee had lived across the street from Barbara Stern and Jack for over ten years and a friendship had developed, partly because of Barbara's background as a nurse. The Doctor had a small clinic next to the Long Beach Hospital. Margaret dunked the toast and tasted the soup hesitantly, while Barbara was on the phone. "Get your coat on, we're going over to the Clinic. I'll get the car."

Dr. McBee checked Margaret, asked when the baby was due, took her pulse and temperature and spent a long time listening to her lungs. "Have you been eating? Have you been taking your vitamins?"

Margaret tried to speak, her voice hoarse, "Those pink and blue things…I tried but I can't swallow them or they come back up. No, I haven't taken them for a while. Are pregnant women always so tired? Have I gained too much weight? I feel huge."

Looking at the thermometer, Dr. McBee answered, "I'd like to put you in my hospital overnight, just for observation and to get some vitamins in you. A hot meal and a good night's sleep is what you need most."

Margaret lay back on the table and closed her eyes. In a small trembling voice she said, "If it's all right with Barbara."

Dr. McBee turned to Barbara, "Barb, I don't like the sound of her lungs. It seems hard for her to breathe, and we need to stop the coughing. I think she should stay overnight...so if you agree, you can just walk her over to the Emergency Door. I will call ahead." It was agreed and the two walked across the street to check Margaret in. The nurses bundled her up in two gowns and a hospital robe. They propped her up against two pillows and brought her a vitamin cocktail which was orange juice thick with honey and waited until she drank it all. Dinner was delivered a short time later, but before she could finish, she was fast asleep.

During the night Margaret had a dream that made her happy. Her family was all together at a picnic in the huge, grassy backyard of their farmhouse in Montana. She could see it as if in a picture frame. Over their heads, white birds were flying up into a blue sky. Covering the hill with a mass of lush green was a cornfield, with huge ears of corn, with red-gold silks peeking out. Margaret and her younger sister were on a blanket with their mother who was handing out sandwiches wrapped in wax paper. Her two bright haired younger brothers were laughing, squinting against the sun and jostling to catch the football their father was throwing to them. On another blanket was Margaret as well, holding a squirming child. The toddler slipped out of her grasp and tottered toward the other blanket, holding out his arms.

She slept deeply all night and felt better, waking with a small cramp in her stomach. She figured it must have been the meatloaf and swung her legs to the edge of the bed to go to the bathroom. Before Margaret could get out of bed, she felt warm wetness puddle under her. The nurse just coming in heard her exclaim, took one look, and started quickly buzzing the nurse's station repeatedly. "Call Dr. McBee...we have a baby coming."

A two-hour labor ended with a huge cramp and a coughing spell, and Margaret Stern's baby was born. That evening, Barbara sat on the side of the bed with a wide smile on her face. "Well, you did it, Margaret. That wasn't so bad, was it?"

Margaret looked down at her son wrapped in blue, sleeping peacefully in her arms. "He was sure in a hurry; I wish Jack could have been here." Kissing her son's soft head, sighing, "He is beautiful, but so little."

The nurse came in with the doctor right behind, "Visiting time is almost over."

Barbara got up and patted Dr. McBee on the back, "Thanks, Doc, for my grandson."

Margaret spoke anxiously to the doctor, "Are all babies this small when they are first born?"

Dr. McBee looked at the nurse and said, "Leave the baby for a few minutes; I need to talk to Margaret. Margaret, when will your husband's ship be in port?"

Margaret smiled, "Is this Thursday? He should be here Sunday morning. He will be so proud. He wanted a boy. Last time he came home, he brought a football. We didn't even know it would be a boy."

Taking the blankets away from the sleeping baby, Dr. McBee spoke carefully, "Margaret, I need to talk to you seriously, and I think we should do it now and not wait. Barbara, I want you to hear this too. Yes, he is small, but he will grow, maybe not as fast as other children. This is just a symptom of something else." Taking a deep breath, she continued, "Most people look at life as if nothing bad will ever happen. But it does, and once in a while it happens to you." She touched the baby's right hand, prying his fingers open, but the little fingers fell right back into a tiny fist. "See how the plates in his forehead are enlarged? I have checked him over thoroughly two times, and the answer is the same. It is something with a long name and it is not good. What he has is not a sickness or a disorder or a disease that can be cured, but to put it honestly, he has a birth defect. He may not grow like other children. It will not go away and this may sound harsh, but it could get worse."

Margaret's hands flew to her face, her eyes filled with tears, "What do you mean? Are you sure? How did this happen? Was it me?"

"I honestly don't know. It was nothing you did. There are so many conflicting opinions. It could be a faulty chromosome that follows family genes, buried for generations. There are so many types of defects, doctors cannot always know.

In a small voice, Margaret whispered, "Will he die?" She touched his small face.

Tucking her head to her chest, Dr. McBee answered, "To be honest, Margaret, maybe, and it could be sooner than we expect. Right now, he is healthy and he is your baby. He is just different. Live your normal life. Be his Mom and love him. He needs you. We can only take care of him the best we can, and see how he grows and develops."

Through all of this Barbara Stern sat white-faced and grim, shaking her head from side to side. Dr. McBee put one hand on Barbara's shoulder and one hand on Margaret's shoulder.

"You have a good support system. He needs a little more attention and we will go into that. I want to keep him for a little while, maybe a week, while he gains some weight. You can go home when your husband gets here."

Barbara drove home, unseeing. When she arrived she began searching the upper kitchen cupboards for a bottle of some kind; anything alcoholic. It was time for a drink. Finding a dusty half bottle of bourbon, she poured a water glass half-full, added ice, then went to the big chair in the living room and sat there for a very long time sipping and looking out the window. Finishing her drink, Barbara went in her bedroom, kneeling in front of her dresser. She pulled out the bottom drawer where she kept her important papers in an old tin box. From it, she lifted a fat manila envelope, pouring the contents onto the floor. In it were the adoption papers of Baby Boy Marisaw, dated twenty -one years ago, the original birth certificate and a newer second birth certificate. She picked up the colorful State of California birth certificate renaming her son 'John Robert Stern', and put it back in the box. She read over the original birth papers as she had dozens of times, reading the mother's name, 'Minnie Marisaw, race – white, age- 24, birthplace – Russia, Trade, profession or particular kind of work done – Circus performer, Business or Industry – Marisaw's Wee Folk Carnival. Father – unknown.

Resolutely, she gathered the rest of the papers from the floor, stumbled into the living room and threw them all in the fireplace. With shaking hands, she lit match after match until the thin, flaky papers caught fire, slowly at first. She watched grimly as they burned brightly until all that was left were grey ashes.

Chapter 10

BABY JACK – 1967

Jack stood with his hands on his wife's shoulders in front of the incubator. He had hitched a ride from the Navy base to meet Margaret at the hospital. Perspiring and breathing heavily, excitement pulsed through his body. He was a father! He swelled with pride and delight. A son! His happiness began to dissolve when he saw the tiny shape with an enlarged head, high forehead and its projecting bumps of bones over the eyes. Jack bit his lip and wrinkling his brow, searched the other bassinets behind the big glass window.

"Is that our baby?"

Margaret answered proudly, "Yes…that is our son. I was there. I want to name him after you."

"What is wrong with his head? It looks big… and crooked. Will he grow out of that?"

Margaret ignored his question replying, "We can't take him home yet. He is too small. The doctor wants to talk to you. She is in her office, you go on in and I will get us some coffee."

Fifteen minutes later Jack walked out of the doctor's office white faced, his eyes wide with alarm.

Pushing the coffee aside, he said roughly, "Let's go home." Margaret touched him on the arm but he pulled away. The ride home was silent; they parked in front of his mother's duplex where they lived.

Jack said, "What went wrong? You should have gone to the Navy Hospital." "Doctor's don't know – it just happens once in a while. The bones aren't right. It is not my fault, or his fault, he is just a baby. We made him on our honeymoon. I love him. I love you. Come in, I'll make lunch."

"What's condo-playsee anyway? Will it get better and go away?"

Margaret made a little sound in her throat, speaking softly, "It's called 'achondroplaysia, and it's a mixed up gene that could cause him not to grow right. It's nobody's fault."

When Barbara came out on the porch and hugged her son, Jack started sobbing on her shoulder, "Mom, Mom, the baby, he's not right. There is something wrong, really wrong. What are we going to do?"

"Oh son, there is nothing you can do right now, not today. Whatever is decided will have to be between you and Margaret. I know what I would do, but I can't get involved."

Margaret put three egg salad sandwiches on the table. "Sit down Jack, eat your lunch. Egg salad is your favorite."

Barbara took her plate and said, "You two have lunch together, you have things to talk about. I am going next door to see Bernice. She wants to talk about her trip. She is leaving next month, moving out to take a job in Mexico." Barbara walked to the other side of the duplex to see her longtime friend and renter, Bernice Davis. Bored and wanting to work after her retirement as an Army nurse in World War II, an employment agency had found Bernice a job. She was leaving to take a job as cook-companion to an older man who was building a beautiful home overlooking a lake in Mexico. Barbara could talk about the baby with her old friend.

The sandwich stuck in Jack's throat. "I can't eat, I can't even think. What are we going to do? He is not normal. You can see that. Kids will laugh and call him a freak. What will my friends say? We can't keep him Margaret. We can't keep him."

Margaret stared at her husband in disbelief. "What on earth do you mean? Of course we will keep him, he is our son. You just don't give babies back. He will come home, live with us and grow up just like anyone else. You will get used to it. After a while you won't even see it."

Jack was insistent, "No! I won't. Maybe you can, but I just…can't. I don't want to talk about this anymore. I'm going back to the Base." Shock and frustration raced through Margaret. Unconsciously, her hand flew up and delivered a stinging slap to her husband's face. Jumping up, he jammed his hat on his head and stormed out the door, slamming it behind him.

Tears sprang to Margaret's eyes, sobs catching in her throat, "Jack, don't leave, I'm sorry. Don't leave us. I love you. I need you, we both need you. We're a family."

Jack got off the bus at Ocean Boulevard and headed for his old haunt, the familiar Sub Room. His face flushed and unsmiling, he spoke to the bartender, "Hey Vince, beer and a shot. Ricky been in?"

"Nah, she's probably not up yet. What do you want with a hooker at noon?"

"I just want to tell her something. I – we – my wife just had a baby."

"Congrats sailor. Have a drink on the house."

Red haired Ricky strolled in just before dark in tight capri pants and a skimpy halter-top with a great amount of white skin bulging over the top. "Hi Vince, hi guys. What's new?"

"Jack, over there, the one sleeping, wants to talk to you. He can't stay here."

Ricky shook him awake. Jack smiled a lopsided smile, "Hi Ricky, remember me? Can I stay with you tonight? I had a fight with my wife and I can't go home. I'll pay."

Ricky calculated how much more she needed for the blue Sears bicycle for her son's 8th birthday and the shipping charges to Palm Springs, where he lived with his grandmother.

"I don't take men to my place, but if I do, it costs. It would be ten for sleeping over and ten for the screw even if we don't, that's it. You can sleep in my car until I'm ready."

"Done. Nothing to think about, Thanks." Jack walked around the block to the parking lot. He sat in the car and thought about the new baby and the big plans he had made for a son. Laying his head down on the seat, he began to cry, and cried until he was exhausted and then began to hiccup. He needed some air, and he needed to call his Mom. Jack called home from a phone booth and Margaret answered.

"Sorry, I left in such a hurry Margaret. I don't know what to do right now, about the baby, I mean. We should think about what to do with him."

Margaret answered coldly, "I don't know what you mean. We are not going to do anything with him. No, Jack, never. This is our child. This is my child. He stays with me. He needs me. My answer to that will always be no, absolutely no!"

Jack was at sea for a week. On his return he called the house from the Base. His Mother answered and Jack spoke quickly, "Mom just listen, let me talk. I can't talk to Margaret. I don't know what to do but I've been thinking. There is talk coming down about closing down the Terminal Island Navy Base here. I'm going to sign up for overseas duty for the next two years, and probably four more after that. I think I could get based in San Diego. Tell Margaret I will put the baby on my allotment for now. I still think she should have him checked at the Navy Hospital. Write to me, Ma. I will come home when I can. You do whatever you think best about the baby and tell Margaret it was me that said it."

The next day Barbara spoke to Margaret. "Jack called and we had a long talk. He thinks it would be best for you and the baby if you put him in a home for special children where they know what to do with babies like him. The sooner the better, before you get attached. If you try to take care of him alone, you are letting yourself in for a lot of heartache. You and Jack will have another child."

Margaret stared stone-faced at her mother in law, then turned away angrily, rushing down the steps to the basement bedroom where her baby slept in peace and quiet. The wall of fierce protectiveness given to mothers and animals since the beginning of time was rock hard and unyielding. Margaret started a letter to her mother in Montana, then tore it up, started another one and tore that one up too. Instead, she wrote a short postcard,

"Mother and Dad: You have a new grandson. I call him Jackie. He has the bluest eyes. We are both doing fine. If you are going to send anything for him, send money, as I need to buy him a crib soon. Lots of sun here. Miss you. Margaret."

Bernice borrowed Barbara's car and drove Margaret and the baby to Dr. McBee's clinic for Jackie's four week checkup. The doctor reminded her to keep a pillow under his head all the time. After handing the gurgling baby to Margaret, she put her arm around them.

"Margaret, I know she has good intentions, but I need to tell you that your mother in law has asked me for a list of State run hospitals and institutions for retarded and special needs children. Are you thinking of that at all?"

Margaret's head jerked up and she shook it from side to side. "No, I am not. Thanks for telling me." A lightning bolt of anger shook Margaret. She let it grow and take over. He was her child, a small bit of her body, her chance to be his mother that someone was trying to take from her. Frustration grew into a white-hot rage, which she tucked away in a corner of her head, bright and strong. She needed to have that strength for their life ahead. Then the sadness came for the child who would never grow. Sorrow filled the roof of her mouth and slid down her throat in a wide, black river spreading darkly full throughout her lungs and rolling through her belly like thick syrup, boiling to the ends of her fingers. It burdened her legs and her body bent forward with its intensity. There was no thought possible as its violence crippled her body. Her mouth opened in a silent scream and tears ran noiselessly down her face. When she thought she could stand no more it faded, leaving her dull and exhausted.

Margaret was white faced and silent on the ride home. Bernie pulled into a fast food restaurant and parked. "Let's get some ice cream and you can tell me what is going on."

Sunday dinner was a ritual with Betty Stern and Bernice was always invited.

Margaret picked at her plate of fried chicken, mashed potatoes and green peas, not joining in the conversation. Barbara asked who wanted pie, as she headed into the kitchen. Bernice looked fixedly at Margaret and said,

"You're not very happy, are you?"

Choking back tears, Margaret answered, "No, but I don't know what to do or where to go. I can't go back to Montana."

"You could always go with me and I could help you with the baby. I was a nurse, you know, for a long time."

"I don't think so, Bernice, but thank you, anyway."

Weeks later, taking the bus this time from the Base hospital and their check up on the baby, Margaret made the decision that had been constantly circling in her head. For as long as she could remember, her hazy picture of joy and happiness included married life with babies. This was not going to be taken from her.

Clutching her son, she stood motionless in front of the other side of the duplex. Burying her face in the baby's soft neck, she breathed in the familiar scent of baby oil and sweet powder. A huge step could be taken that would end all discussion about the baby's care. Straightening her back decisively, she knocked at Bernice's door.

"Bernice, I want to go with you to Mexico."

Chapter 11

A DAY IN MAY – 1969

CARMEN'S BACK YARD

It began as any other day. Margaret woke to the smell of coffee and muted sounds from the other house. She could hear Carmen calling in the kitchen. Carmen was a Sunday cook at a restaurant she and Bernie had discovered soon after their arrival. Margaret had seen a tiny sign on the restaurant wall and jumped at the opportunity to clean up and live in a small house in Carmen and Manny's backyard. The door banged behind Manny, and Luis was not far behind his uncle, running down the hill swinging their lunchboxes. They couldn't be late to meet the pickup truck at the corner which took them to their jobs at the tile yard in Jocotopec.

Glancing at her watch, Margaret took out one tray of cookies and put in another. Plenty of time to get dressed, wake Jackie and get him ready for the day. She was working at the Casa Redondo motel office that day so Dolores, the motel owner, could go to Guadalajara to have lunch with friends and shop, which could take all day. Carmen would watch Jackie and he would play with Ruby, Carmen's small daughter, though Ruby, at four years old, did all the talking and playing. Margaret took care of Ruby on Sundays when Carmen stood behind the buffet to cook omelets and waffles for the Gallo Loco restaurant. Ruby could not say Margaret – so she had become Maigret. She stepped outside with her coffee mug, breathing in the fragrant air and accepted the promise of another beautiful day. She sat quietly outside her casita in the morning sun, enjoying the brilliance of the bougainvillea. Ribbons of sunbeams dropped through the branches in spotty pictures. In one look, she could see palm trees next to fir trees, a burdened lime tree and the wide branches of a flourishing avocado tree, colorful flowers of all kinds, reds, pinks, yellows, swift small birds with black mask and white underbellies moving in a cloud together, and a lizard motionless on a rock. She loved to walk on the grass-like clover and tend to the pots filled with red and white amaryllis that lined the worn brick walk from the main house. She relished the now familiar scene and with a deep breath of satisfaction thought, that this was where she wanted to be; somewhere where life was slower. She saw a goat and chickens and flowers she had planted around the house she had cleaned and painted. She had her son, kind friends and a peaceful life. She missed her family and sometimes she missed

Jack, but she could not, or would not, go back. This was their home and she was happy.

She thought of Jackie's father somewhere out on some ocean on an aircraft carrier. She welcomed the allotment checks that came sporadically through his mother to her Post Office box. Sighing deeply, the thought skipped through her mind that someday, something official would have to be done. The buzzer on the timer rang and she took the tray out of the oven...peanut butter cookies, an order from the restaurant. She bathed Jackie, dressed and fed him, and broke a cookie in half for his treat.

"Here my big boy. You are almost two, do you know that?" She pulled his cap over his head, hiding the square bones that rose and enlarged his forehead, and tugged a few blond curls around his face. Placing him in the wooden scoop chair that Manny, her landlord, had made so he could half-sit, she buckled the straps firmly. The unintelligible noises, sounds and bubbles he made were his conversation with her. His small arms waved excitedly; he knew he would be going outside. "Okay, cookie face," she said as she backed his seat to the avocado tree trunk facing the kitchen window. "Wave to Carmen; Ruby's coming out now. Kiss Mama bye-bye."

Luis was the first to see the two children on the blanket when he came home from work. Jackie was out of his chair and he and Ruby were on the ground, fast asleep, hand in hand, faces smeared with cookie crumbs. Luis knelt and straightened the blanket and unclasped their hands. Jackie's hand was ice cold and he was not breathing. Worried, Luis picked up the sleeping girl and jogged into the house, calling, "Carmen, CARMEN. Hurry, go to Jackie."

Carmen, Manny and Luis were sitting on the ground near Jackie when Maigret came home. She saw Carmen's red eyes and solemn face first, then the two somber men. Her eyes fixed on her son, who was white-faced and very still. "What's wrong? Is Jackie sick?"

Manny answered, "No, mi Amiga. Sit with us. You will need to be strong for what I tell you. The angels came and took your son to Heaven. He is with Jesus now."

Maigret fell to her knees at his side and whispered, "No – no, not yet," kissing his face and holding him tightly in her arms, as if the heat of her body could warm him. She swayed back and forth with him in her arms, singing quietly,

"Rock a bye baby, in the tree top,
When the wind blows, the cradle will rock.
When the bow breaks, the cradle will fall,
Down will come baby, cradle and all."

Maigret seemed frozen. Her eyes were closed so she could not see them leave her there alone, rocking the body of her son.

Carmen had borrowed all the plastic white chairs from the restaurant for the vigil at her house. The friends and neighbors stayed all night drinking sweet black coffee and praying out loud. Even the smallest guest brought a token gift of flowers. They took turns passing by the small, still body dressed in white, to say goodbye, speaking in hushed tones. He looked to be sleeping with his favorite teddy bear by his side.

The next morning two of the men carried the tiny burden to the nearby cemetery in their small village of Guadalupe while the women who walked behind in the procession, sang the haunting melody, 'Reposar'. Carmen kept her arm around Maigret and repeatedly told her that her son was in a good place now.

Chapter 12

MANNY THE FISHERMAN

Manny woke with a start. It was very early Sunday morning. Slipping out of bed without waking his wife Carmen, adjusting the covers over her, he dressed in the dark. Picking up the lunch his wife had made, he smiled to himself and thought- today I will catch many fish.

After loading his canoe in the pickup, he drove to his favorite spot at the edge of Lake Chapala.

The lake was the largest body of water in Mexico. The edges were high peaks vaguely reminiscent of a volcano crater, which it could have been millions of years ago. Lake Chapala was fed by seasonal rains and mountain springs from four rivers, the main one being the river Lerma, occasionally varying the lake size of sixty miles long and seventeen miles wide. Much of its water raced through a treatment plant into the thirsty faucets of neighboring Guadalajara. No motorboats used this part of the placid lake for sport, and there were no speedboats, water skiing or boisterous play. The boats that used this lake were slim canoes that slid silently across its glassy surface, paddled by a lone angler. Manny looked forward to his Sunday fishing after a long hard work week and to the quiet war between man and fish.

Huge floating islands of brilliant green heart shaped leaves dotted with vivid purple water hyacinth blossoms drifted at a snail's pace from one side of the lake to the other. The roots of the greenery stretched down into the dark and cloudy water in thick and deadly tangles. Herons and fat white pelicans with outlandish beaks rode the islands, waiting, looking for their next meal.

The color of night was different in Mexico; it was deeply black, heavy and warm. Far across the lake was a comforting ribbon of twinkling lights from a small village with an unpronounceable name. Manny's nephew, Luis, had come from there when he was about twelve to live with Manny and Carmen. Manny's widowed brother had remarried and with his two daughters and the two daughters of his new wife, the two bedroom house was bursting at the seams with children. His father decided it would be better for Luis to go to a bigger village where he could go to school and find a job, than to stay with the crowded family and take care of the pig farm.

The sky began to lighten between the ragged peaks, first with a reddish glow, then more red-orange, then yellow brightness peeked between the black hills. The anglers in their canoes sat motionless patiently fishing. One should not look away, as it takes only a moment or two for the huge orange ball to rise and for the warmth of the day to begin.

Shivering, Manny reached for his coffee thermos and took a scalding gulp. He was hoping to catch many fish so his family could have a fish fry that night and the rest he might sell to the restaurant.

Chapter 13

DAY OF THE DEAD FOR CHILDREN

NOVEMBER 1, 1971

Cheery and confident in the doorway, Ruby held out a braided straw crucifix and an armful of peach bellflowers, pink geraniums, red and blue bougainvillea, and dusky marigolds with dirt still clinging to the roots, all definitely just picked from the backyard. "These are for Jackee, for the altar."

Margaret studied the little child. An enchanting picture, her glossy black hair stubbed out on each side of her head with red bands, her tiny hands grasping all the colored flowers and a white sugar candy skull. It had been over two years since two year old Jackie had passed away in his sleep, holding hands with Ruby on the grass.

"What do you mean, Ruby?"

"It is Dia de Los Innocentes today, Maigret. Tonight we go to the graves, and you are coming too.

These are for Jackee, for your table. So we can remember and pray." Ruby propped a cross against the wall and organized the flowers loosely around it. "Put his picture right here," she directed, with six year old authority. "Mama' is baking the bread and I will bring one when they are done. You put that right here by La Calaveras. How do you say it in Engles, scull?" She looked at her handiwork, made the sign of the cross and kissed her thumb, "Reposar, mi amigo, Jackee." Ruby walked back across the yard and passing the hammock patted Luis on the arm.

Luis lazily swung in his hammock on the patio, watching. He had a good view of the doorway of Maigret's casita and had spent many hours swinging, pretending to be asleep, and studying her. He was fifteen four years ago when she had moved in and he became fascinated with her. He had brought her soup when she was sick. He had offered to help her when she planted flowers. He especially liked it when she washed her hair and sat in the sun to let it dry. He had heard her weep many times in the night after her son died, and made up stories about what he would do if she invited him in. Would she let him hold her, would she let him kiss her? Groaning and restless in the swaying hammock, stirrings of teenage desire flickered between his legs.

Chapter 14

THE BONFIRE

AT THE LAKE – 1972

The property owner pushed a three legged stool up against the brick wall of his yard and peered over. He shouted at the dim figures around the bonfire at the edge of the lake.

'Hey you kids, turn off that music and go home. It's after one o'clock in the morning and people are trying to sleep."

A voice from the fire answered, "Go to bed old man, it's not your beach."

"It's not yours either, and if you are not gone in five minutes, I am calling the police. I am counting…and put out that fire."

One of the boys grumbled, "Aw, come on, let's go. We don't want trouble and the beer is all gone." One couple walked down the beach toward the lights of a small village. The music stopped; two cars roared away leaving Luis and his two friends, Erica and

Victor. Victor was sound asleep. Luis turned to walk away and Erica called his name,

"Luis, get me a beer, por favor." She was half reclining next to a snoring Victor. Luis reached down through the few icy splinters in the water and found the last beer at the bottom of the tub. Erica shifted and dropped one knee, opening her legs so that the dying firelight slipped up to the shadowed triangle between her legs. Her fingers cupped one breast and as he handed her the beer can, she said softly, "Do you like what you see?" Luis shoved the can in her hand and quickly walked away.

"Hey, you didn't even open this. Luis! You are stupid – do you hear me? Victor, wake up. I have to go home. Come on, let's go." Victor groaned and sat up,

"I have to pee."

"Pee on the fire - stupid." Erica turned the tub on its side and water sloshed onto the embers of the fire and onto Victor's shoes.

"Dios…you got my shoes wet." He stepped back, stumbled and fell.

"Take me home, Victor. All you do is sleep. You're drunk and you are stupid too. All boys are stupid." She followed him pushing him up the sandy incline.

Luis stood looking out over the dark, secretive water, dragging out the enjoyment of a warm night punctuated by a thousand gleaming stars. He turned his head away from the acrid smell of embers and spilled beer and jogged up the beach. He filled his lungs with the moist, fresh smell of the water, taking pleasure in the small bits of dancing brightness over each curling dark wave. This was his lake. These were his stars. The heady thrill of being a young male caused him to howl as he ran faster and faster on the wet sand. He made his way confidently in the moonlight that flooded the dirt path up past the dim porch light glow of the blue house where Miguel and his mother, Rosa, lived and was glad to see the nightlights of the restaurant. His calves tightened pleasurably as he ran up the cobblestone road towards the streetlight next to his house. Slipping his foot into a hole of broken bricks, he swung himself over the rocky sidewall and dropped down, heading for the large woven hammock where he slept.

"It's me, Carmen. It's Luis. Buena Noches." There was no answer. He took one look at the casita before he closed his eyes, and whispered, "Buena Noches, Maigret." There was no answer. Maybe someday there would be.

Chapter 15

NEW YEAR'S EVE – 1972

Luis stepped out of Carmen's house onto the patio, deeply breathing in the fresh air. The New Year's Eve party inside was heavy with smoke, and haphazard guitars accompanied off key singing, jokes and laughter. Cars were racing up and down the street honking; fireworks had been popping since early in the morning. Friends and relatives were enjoying drinks while waiting for the fireworks over the lake and Carmen's legendary midnight buffet. Fernando, the son of the restaurant owner, was on his way over with his violin. Luis had sat close to Maigret who had left a short time ago. He and Maigret had become good friends over this past year. It was almost midnight and Luis had a plan in mind. He had thought about it for two years and needed Maigret to make it happen.

He walked carefully toward the dimly lit window of her casita, hearing the rustle of the hens in the trees and the bleat of a sleepy goat. He felt warm and good after two, or was it three, tequila shots and a Kahlua and coffee. Tapping on her door with the tips of his fingers, he waited.

It's me, its Luis." There was no answer so he tapped again. There was no answer so he turned the knob and went in. The room was neat and clean and smelled of fresh laundry and sugar. A small table lamp threw its feeble light over Maigret where she had fallen asleep on the couch in her nightgown. Luis knelt and looked intently at her peaceful face.

"Maigret, wake up. I want to talk to you." Maigret woke with a start. "Luis, what's wrong?"

"Nothing is wrong – I just need to talk to you. It's important."

"Let me get a robe." As she struggled to get up, he held her and knelt in front of her.

"Maigret, No – don't. I have seen your body. Remember two years ago when you fell from the roof when you were cleaning. I caught you. I washed your hands and knees and put you to bed. When you were sick with the flu, I fed you soup and aspirina and changed your gown when it was wet. I kept you warm when you were shivering, sleeping next to you on that small bed."

Maigret sat up straight and pulled the afghan around her. "Yes, I remember most of it. You were sixteen and a big help to me. I was in a bad way after Jackie died; thank you."

"That was years ago when I was young. I am older now. I am a man! I...I want to be a man and with you. I've thought of this for a long time. I want us to, for us to..." He put his arm around her shoulders. "Let me say this right. For my first, for my first time with a woman – not just any woman, I just want you. I have waited. I have not done this, or anything, not at school parties, or the bonfires. I thought only of you and waited for the right time. I held you when you were sick. I felt your body next to me and knew you were the one. This is the right time, you are the woman."

She shook her head and took his arm away from her, "No, you're just a boy."

"I watched you dry your hair in the sun. I wanted to touch your hair. I want to touch your hair now."

"No, that would not be good."

"I looked at your legs when I was painting the rocks in your yard. I wanted to touch your legs. I want to touch your legs now."

Her voice was faint, "No, no. I don't want you to. "

He took her hand and kissed it, sliding his hands up her arm, saying softly. "I think of you every morning when I wake up and every night when I go to sleep. I see your face in my dreams. I am a man now and have a man's feelings. I want this, and I want you. Give this to me, Maigret, this is mine."

Maigret looked at his solemn face and shook her head knowing that it would be a big mistake. She thought back over the time she had spent with his family and of their kindness to her and of Luis as a friend. The low lights, the drinks she had and his constant soothing voice, the touch of his warm hands all created a flicker of yearning that she hardly remembered having. She thought she had forgotten those feelings.

Fireworks and shouts began outside. Luis urged, "Kiss me Happy New Year, Maigret."

Just then, the sound of Fernando's violin soared through the night with a pure and thrilling melody the filled the air with passionate intensity. Maigret rose from the couch, the afghan dropped, and Luis stood beside her.

"No Luis, it would not be right. I must be crazy to even think about it." She kissed him softly and could taste the sweetness of Kahlua. His body pressed against hers as he took her hand and placed it between his legs. He was warm and hard; a small sigh escaped her lips.

His insistent voice was husky in her ear, "Give me this, Maigret, one time, my first. It is important that you be the one. " The kiss deepened and his tongue touched hers…a spark flashed. The longing grew in her, the smell and feel of him with his arms around her was compelling. She had missed the feeling of body to body closeness. A minute passed, then another. His arms tightened and his body warmth melted her loneliness.

Slowly, Maigret slipped her hand under his shirt. The feel of his skin was rich and creamy; she wanted to touch him again. She opened her mouth to let him in further.

He gathered her to him, turned her to the bedroom and said into her mouth, "Show me."

Next morning the rooster calling from the bay tree woke Maigret and she stiffened. She could feel warm breath on the back of her neck and the memory of last night came flooding back to her with the alarming thought that he should not be there. Luis stirred and slid his hand down her back to her waist. For a breathless moment, their bodies tangled together.

Maigret turned in the narrow bed, "You can't be here. This is wrong. What if someone sees you? Get up. You know there will be trouble. You must go before its light."

He kissed her nose, "Have you forgotten me so soon? I can't forget you. I will never forget this night. Let me see you, all of you." He threw the blanket off of them both.

"You are beautiful. Kiss me, just once."

Maigret got up, leaned down and brushed her lips across his, "Dress quickly, and then go, before it is daylight. Go!"

In quick movements, he was dressed and at the door, shoes in hand and he whispered unsteadily, "When can I see you? Can I come to you again?"

"I don't know, just go." She closed the door behind him and slipped back under the still warm, tangled blankets. Closing her eyes, she drifted back to sleep not wanting to think about all that now.

Chapter 16

FEAST OF KINGS

January 6, 1973

All week after New Year's Eve is the Festival of the Feast of Kings. Manny, Carmen, and all the family and neighbors were planning to go to the nearby village of Cajitlan for the last night of the Festival to honor the Three Kings, the Magi and their procession. It was always a huge event with many stalls selling food, beverages and wares. There would be games, dancing, and, of course, fireworks at night. Pilgrims would come from miles around to light candles, to pray for their children and touch the robes of the Magi for good fortune.

Maigret did not go, and half expected the soft knock on her door. Luis took her hands first, holding her close. She could feel his legs shaking. She heard the question in his voice as he spoke her name. In response, she pressed tight against him. His hand moved under her dress. caressing her bare skin. A vivid image of their bodies close together filled her head. This time, Maigret turned to the bedroom. They spent the day in bed pleasantly discovering each other again in the half-light that peeped through the small slatted window. Maigret marveled at his lean body and the smooth texture of his skin. She rose naked, to his admiring astonishment, to fill plates with avocados, crackers and the previous day's roasted chicken, carrying them back to their nest of blankets.

"When do you think they will be home?" asked Maigret.

"They will stay for the fireworks. When I hear their car, I will go to the hammock."

A week later, Manny and Luis jumped off the back of the truck bed at the corner near the El Gallo Loco. At nineteen, Luis was the youngest of the group, but he worked along seasoned tile makers and put in a full day at the tile yard. Every afternoon, tired and covered with dust, they stopped at the Gallo Loco for iced tea.

The resident in number six at the motel, was standing outside his teardrop trailer which was parked behind his room. Tall and slender, hands on hips, he was staring down at a pile of clothing and magazines, his thin chest pumping hard.

He called across the courtyard, "Son, could you come and help me for a minute?" Luis drank from his frosty glass, crunching on ice cubes, and then went to him.

"I want to get this mattress out, not the pad, just turn that over." Together, they twisted and turned the single mattress out of the small door, tugging it out dropping it on the ground. "Thank you. Can you reach those boxes up on the shelf? They are full of books...could be heavy. Good job. Gracias. My name is Charles, call me Charlie. What's yours?"

"I'm Luis. Que pasa? Cleaning house?" quizzed Louis.

"Sort of...I want to paint the inside. What color should it be?

Luis scratched his head, "I don't know, white?"

"That's sounds good. Can I hire you to paint it? Shouldn't take but a day. My son is coming down from Texas and I want it looking good." Then he began coughing and could not stop. He leaned against the motel wall and then half fell down hard on a stool. His face was grey, and when he could speak, his lips twisted into a thin smile, saying, and "Guess I could be taking my dirt nap any day now."

Luis responded, "I could start on Saturday and finish on Sunday." The two men shook hands, agreeing on the job. Luis finished painting Sunday afternoon, closed the paint cans and was washing his brushes while Charlie was inspecting the trailer. Looking up across the walkway, Luis saw Maigret enter the motel office and Dolores, the owner, get in her car and leave.

He wondered if she had seen him. His breath strangled in his chest. He had to see her; but how? The people eating on the restaurant patio would see him go in.

Just then Maigret came out of the office with an armful of sheets and towels and went into room Number four.

Charlie took out his wallet, "Good job, Luis. Let me pay you."

"Gracias, Charlie, I will work for you anytime." Seemingly calm, Luis was thinking feverishly, did she see me? Ah, she is so beautiful. I remember the curve of her hip, the soft skin of her breasts. Does she think of me?

Charlie handed Luis money, stroking his chin. "Thanks. I appreciate it. Sorry to say, I may be moving on." Charlie was talking but Luis couldn't hear him. He wanted his arms around her, to lay on her and push inside her, to hear her call his name. His choice was made. Luis stood, looking straight ahead, walked slowly around the trailer to the back of the motel, and tapped on the back window of Number four until it opened.

The following Friday, Carmen was helping with the afternoon shift at the restaurant. Manny was taking all the family down for a late lunch and asked Maigret if she would like to come.

"Thanks, but no, I'm baking shortcakes for the restaurant for tomorrow."

Luis ate very little, and then said he was going home. Racing up the hill, he jumped the wall and called in a low voice, "Maigret, open." She opened the door and smiled at his earnest face.

She held out her arms saying, "This is no good, you know. This has to stop, someone will find out."

He backed her into the bedroom, whispering, "I adore you. I need you. Tell me you want me." He pushed her gently back on the bed, bearing his weight on his arms, and raining light kisses all over her face. As he moved into her, she sighed and tightened her arms around him. She quickly moved up to meet him; his impatience excited her.

Juana and Carmen closed the restaurant, and the family walked home in the half-dark, Ruby running on ahead. Carmen was bringing in the sheets and towels from the laundry line, and thought she heard a small cry in the casita, and stepped closer. Hearing two voices, she stood straight and still, not wanting to understand. Bundling the basket hurriedly, with sheets trailing, she said, "Manny, husband, I think the goat is untied, would you go out and see?"

"Ah, no, I am tired. Ruby will go."

"No, Papa, you must go. Just go out and smoke. Do this for me?" She spoke firmly, with her hands on her hips.

Manny sighed and did as she said. He sat in the hammock and smoked. Soon the door to the casita opened, and in the glow of the small lamp, he could see the two figures kissing. Manny jumped up, throwing his cigarette on the ground. Shocked, glaring wide eyed, he began shouting at Luis in anger and disbelief,

'WHAT IS THIS? I see it with my own two eyes! Do you bring shame to my house? Do not lie. I raised you as my son and you stab me in the back. This is a sin in God's eyes."

Surprised, Luis jerked free from Maigret's embrace and ran toward his uncle, his features molding into a mask of apology.

"Manny… Tio… Uncle. I am sorry. I am sorry. It is not her fault. I went to her. What can I do? I love her. We could marry."

Manny drew himself up to his full height, his face red with rage and put his face close to his nephew's, staring intensely and shouting, "This is ended. ENDED! You will not speak to her again. She must go. Go in the house. I must think." Spittle was spraying and running down his chin. He turned on his heel and savagely tore the hammock from its posts.

Maigret had closed the door, standing with her back against it, her heart pounding. "Damn, oh damn. I should have known. What am I going to do now?"

The two men went to work as usual the next morning in silence. Manny did not get on the truck after work, and said that he was going to visit friends and would be late for supper. Manny went to the house of Hector Sandoval, who had been his good friend and neighbor for many years before moving to Jocotopec for a better job. Their children had gone to school together and the families had been great friends. Sweet and pretty Teresa Sandoval, now in high school, had been a dance partner to Luis in grade school.

"Hector, we must have a serious talk." A tequila bottle half full was in the center of the table with limes cut in quarters and a plate of salt. Manny asked his friend how he liked his new job as a teacher. Hector in turn asked how Manny was getting along at the brickyard and how his nephew was keeping up with the work. Manny inquired about the family, the wife and three girls. They sipped tequila with salt. Manny explained that Luis was fully grown and wanted to be on his own and wondered if Teresa would be at the plaza the next Sunday evening to walk in the group of young ladies as was the custom for young people. The men walked the opposite way and showed their interest by offering a flower to their choice and if it was accepted, then they walked together. Manny crossed his fingers behind his back and said,

"Luis has mentioned he would like to see Teresa again."

Hector sat up straight and smiled broadly, "Yes, yes, she still talks about him...I will be sure she is there."

The two men talked for an hour or more. When the bottle was empty, they stood up, embraced, shook hands solemnly and said goodbye.

Manny ate the dinner kept warm in the oven for him. He spoke to Luis without looking at him, "From tonight on, you will sleep in the house. Tomorrow is Saturday, and Juana at the restaurant needs help in her garden. You will take the two bags of goat manure to her and work there until dark. On Sunday you will go to church, sit with me, and think about what you have done. You will need to say many prayers. You have been like a son to me for eight years and my heart is heavy. You will not put shame on this house again. In the afternoon, we will go to the plaza in Jocotopec and you will walk the circle with the rest of the young people. When Teresa Sandoval, who for some reason still has feelings for you, passes, you will give her a flower. This is how it will be…and she is who you will marry. You have a choice: do this, what I say, or get on the bus right now and go back to the other side of the lake to your father's pig farm. I have no other words."

Luis nodded his head and covered his troubled face with his hands, "It will be as you say, Uncle."

LINDA

Chapter 17

BACK TO THE SUNDAY BRUNCH – 1980

Linda Lou looked up with tears in her eyes, her voice slurring, "Well, I am not even sure where I am. This nice woman sat next to me on the plane and listened to my story, and I was crying the whole time. She brought me here in her taxi, to rest a while. That was Dolores, the owner of the motel."

"I had a happy life until just lately. My mother, her name was Betty, had this idea in her head when I was a baby that I would end up in Hollywood. She put me in my first beauty contest when I was nine months old. I don't remember that, of course. We went everywhere, to all kinds of fairs and pageants, and she made it fun. I won trophies, and money, crowns and ribbons and a lot of other stuff. I did lots of pageants. I did a lot of modeling. She said I was wonderful, that I was going to go right to the top. Then she got sick and died in San Francisco when I was twenty. She was the best mother. I could have been queen of another pageant if it hadn't been for what happened last week." Linda sobbed and wiped her eyes on her napkin. "She told me these stories so many times I can almost hear her saying the words. This all happened in Kansas City where we used to live."

Betty Campbell searched the reader board in the lobby of the old building. She had checked the address three times, and this was it. The Blue Ribbon Talent Agency, Room 303. She would never come to this part of town unless it was for something important like this. She looked around: the floors needed sweeping and the linoleum was wearing off the stair steps. Adjusting the wiggling three year old to the other hip, she pushed the button and stepped into the elevator. She looked straight ahead, ignoring the cracked mirrors taped with silver duct tape. When she got off on the third floor, a strong odor of burnt coffee filled her nose, not quite covering the smell of mildew.

She had entered Linda Lou in three baby picture contests and four pageants in the last two years. The winnings consisted of two pair of shoes in the 'Walk in my Shoes' contest at Parsons Shoe Mill, a $25.00 savings bond for the 'Fourth of July Baby' contest, movie tickets, a $10.00 grocery credit, and $75.00 to open a bank account. She had opened it and closed it the next day. Betty felt they should be doing better. In the packets about the last two contests was a bright blue postcard with a picture of Shirley Temple with the announcement:

"Even Shirley had to start somewhere. Call us for the best results.

We need babies and children for pictures, catalog models, commercials

And movies. We have our own professional photographer. Nominal fee."

Betty stood a moment and read the words on the door,

"BLUE RIBBON TALENT AGENCY"

Betty pushed the door open and was greeted by a cloud of cigarette smoke curling up from the ashtray of a thin woman with brown hair in waves like that of an old time movie star. She didn't stop filing her fingernails and instead stated flatly,

"Can I help you? Nobody is in today – just me. If you want to see Abe, you have to come back. If you want to sign up, I can do that."

Betty put Linda Lou down and handed her the blue card, "This is what I came about. What do you mean sign up?

Miss Brown Hair put down her fingernail file and began to speak as if rehearsed, "You sign up with me and the kid gets her picture taken. Then Mr. Gladman shops around and finds the jobs. It's ten bucks a year to join, but that doesn't include the professional picture. We are a talent agency, just like in the movies. Take a look at the wall. See those pictures? Those are some of our members."

Betty's eyes opened wide at the array of smiling babies, fresh faced boys and girls, some with curly hair, some with straight hair, some held stuffed toys, umbrellas, hats or purses. 'I do want to join. Will she get jobs? What kind of jobs? What about the picture?"

Miss Brown Hair pulled out a worn receipt book and began to write. "I'll make your appointment for next Friday after lunch to come back for the picture. That will be ten dollars please.'

Next Friday after lunch Betty and Linda Lou waited patiently in the outer room of the agency, and finally Abe Gladman came bustling out of his office. He was a big man, who wore a loose Hawaiian shirt to cover his bulging stomach. His head was very shiny; what little hair he had was combed over to one side to make the most of it. With a big practiced grin, he extended his hand,

"I am Abe Gladman and I am glad to see you, glad to meet you. And who do we have here? What a nice little kid. What a pretty little kid." Kneeling down on one knee in front of Linda Lou, he said, "My name is Abe, what's yours?"

Linda Lou looked at her mother. Betty patted her shoulder, Say your name, honey, like I told you. Do your strut, do the turn and walk back."

"My name is Linda Lou Campbell." Taking the sides of her little A-line dress in her hands, she stood up straight, strolled to the end of the room, looked over her shoulder and smiled, turned on one foot and curtsied.

Abe boomed, "Let's get started. Come on in." Abe's office was big and airy, and in one corner was a dollhouse, big enough for a child to play in. There were two tricycles, toys, a rocking horse, and a wall of painted characters with hats on hooks over their heads. Abe stacked up some loose photos on a corner table and picked up a small camera. "Let's sit here and talk about what we are going to do. She can play in the playhouse. First, let me take a picture of you two. Does she mind having her picture taken?"

"Oh, no, she is used to it. She loves having her picture taken, don't you Linda?"

Abe took the photo of them close together as Linda was peeking at the dollhouse. "Here, you take the rest of the roll while she plays. I will use my Polaroid and take pictures from over here. We'll get some great shots. Okay, honey, you go play inside the playhouse. Open the little gate, walk around, go in and look out the windows so we can see you and take your picture. We need to take lots of pictures."

Betty coaxed Linda Lou to pose and smile, in the house looking out the little window, on the tricycle and petting the rocking horse. Abe hummed quietly as he walked around the room, clicking. Betty's camera stopped and rolled back. She glumly put it down saying,

"That was fun, thanks."

"Ah, don't thank me, this is business, this is business. You are helping your little gal here on her way. Some of these will be just fine…our next stop is getting her in front of a professional photographer. A professional. He is here every other Saturday and will do the head shots for her book. She needs a book of photos. Make an appointment for a week from tomorrow in the afternoon. His photos only cost $5.00." Pointing out the window, he continued, "See that Rexall Drugstore on the corner? Help me out by dropping your roll of film there to my account, and we will have it when you come back." Dropping to one knee again in front of Linda Lou, he said, "So long for now, sweetheart. You are a nice little kid, a pretty little kid."

The next Saturday, Jay James, lugged his heavy black suitcase out of the elevator and into the Blue Ribbon Talent Agency. It took two trips to bring his equipment up from his photography business across the street. Jay was the best. A small, thin man, he made the children comfortable. He had the gift of clicking the camera at just the right time, and could always catch the big smile, the tilt of the head, the pensive child, and the tiny tear in the eye. Even the most obstinate child came away as perfection through his lens.

"Jay, this is the one. This is the one, I just know it. This one is going places. Do your best stuff for this little kiddie. Here they are. Mom, come on in and meet the photographer. He is a real professional. Take your girl over to the playhouse and just let her play. She won't even notice Jay. You and I can sit back here out of the way."

Betty watched the photographer set the lighting, and then disappear under the black hood. In a moment, he raised a bunny rabbit with floppy ears on a long stick above his head saying, "Hewwo, I'm Bugs Bunny, who are you?" Linda Lou giggled and said her name. Click. She pointed at the rabbit and laughed. Click. She got on the smaller tricycle and rode in a circle. Click. She petted the rag mop mane of the rocking horse. Click. She went into the playhouse, put her arms on the windowsill, and smiled at the wagging rabbit. Click. Jay smiled and said, "That's the money shot, right there. Let's be sure…just one more."

Abe, wiping perspiration from his face, said to Linda Lou. "Can you do a somersault?
How about a somersault for me sweetheart, over to your Mom. Can you do that?"

Linda Lou opened the picket fence gate and somersaulted across the room, holding the last one. A picture of sturdy pink legs and frilly white panties filled the lens. Click. Abe sighed and knew that was the money shot for his album. He closed his eyes and pictured the locked bottom drawer in his desk with the thick photo album of the very select 8 x 10 glossies he indulged in at certain times with a secret pleasure that only he could give himself.

Chapter 18

DIXIE DINER, ROSEBURG – 1955

Little Miss Douglas County, Junior Division, was sound asleep in the back seat of the 1955 Chevrolet, driven by Mr. Perry Borders. He had been a customer and Betty had served him chicken fried steak at the Dixie Diner in Roseburg. Betty's old car had wheezed its last in Denver, so they had luckily hitched a ride with a man and wife team driving a truck bound for the Veteran's Hospital in Roseburg. Betty had worked at the diner for ten days taking one day off to enter Linda into the local County Fair Pageant. In a frothy pink second hand dress, five year old Linda Lou had won easily. First prize was a gold paper crown and $50.00…which would help on their trip to California. During his pie and ice cream, Perry had mentioned that he was traveling south to Red Bluff. Betty's ears perked up and she hurried over to pour more coffee.

"I'm going to Hollywood myself, that is, my girl and I. How far is Red Bluff from here?"

Perry shook his head, "Let's see, Roseburg to Red Bluff, my guess as the crow flies about 250 miles, three or four hours"

Biting her fingernails, Betty asked, "How far is Red Bluff from Hollywood?"

Stroking his chin, Perry took a couple of minutes before answering, "Well, not looking at a map, I'd have to guess it's quite a ways, maybe six or seven hundred miles. I'm not going that far."

Betty thought hard, taking a second hard look at his crew cut, clean cut round face and nice eyes behind his glasses. She leaned over and whispered, accentuating what slight southern drawl she had, "If ah pay for your gas, would you let us ride along? I'll buy your dinner here too."

"Oh, you don't have to do that girlie, but to tell the truth, I wouldn't mind the company. I can't wait around though…got to be on my way."

"Let me collect from the couple in the corner and the guy having coffee. I'll be ready by the time you finish your pie." She cleaned efficiently around the coffee drinker. "Special treat for you Mister, the coffee is free if you leave right now. We're closing." Obliging, he took one last gulp and left.

Betty turned the door sign over to show "CLOSED". "Is everything okay folks? Sorry to rush but we are closing."

The couple answered, "No problem, we are done. Here is a ten that should cover it." Betty walked them to the door and turned off the porch lights. Ringing $8.59 into the cash drawer, she kept the tip and counted out her nine days pay. Writing a goodbye note to Dixie, she hung up her apron and called out to the cook,

"Ray, no one is here. The door is locked. I'm leaving. You might as well shut off the stove and go home." She looked over at Perry who smiled and waved as he went out. Betty locked the door after him and checked to see that all the electrical cords were pulled.

"So long Dixie, Hello Red Bluff."

Their tiny sleeping room was a few short steps toward the back of the building. She woke Linda Lou, put her on the toilet while she shoved their few clothes in a cloth bag, then lugged the suitcase filled with plastic covered pageant dresses to the door. It went into the back seat, and their coats with the soft bag next to it made a nest for the sleepy child. Betty settled in next to Perry and headed south down the highway. They talked for a while until Betty laid her head back and nodded off. When she opened her eyes, Perry had his hand on her knee. She shook his hand off as the car pulled up in front of a motel with yellow neon flashing a $10.00 rate. Perry put his hand on her knee again, saying,

"Wake up, Toots, it's almost midnight. We're in Red Bluff. Time to sleep in a real bed."

Betty fished in her purse, "Let me give you $10.00 for our room."

"Never mind now, I'll get it later." He headed toward the lit lobby and returned, handing one key through the window. "We are in luck, they had one room left. Go on in and get settled. I see a bar down the block. I'll just walk down there and get a six pack or two and we'll have us a little party."

Betty stared at the one key and, looking out, could see there was only one other car in the parking lot, and thought to herself, *not so fast, Buster. I ain't a farm girl just off the bus. How do I get out of this?* Dropping the key on the floor, she looked wildly around across the driveway to the gas station. An elderly couple was pulling up to the pumps in a vintage station wagon.

Betty jumped out of the car, ran to the passenger side, and said urgently to the sweet-faced woman, "I need help! See that car over there…my five year old is in there. That man gave us a ride from Roseburg and now he wants us to go in the motel with him. Can you help us get away from here? Oh, please, he is not a nice man."

Hand to her mouth, she responded, "My goodness, my grey head tells me there is an emergency. Now you just bring your baby. We have plenty of room in the back seat. Henry, open the back." One trip brought the pageant suitcase and on the second trip she half ran, carrying Linda, the coats and the clothing. By the time the tank was full, the doors were all closed and

Betty laid her head down on the soft bag next to her daughter.

"Just drive away now Henry, and don't look back. We have us a situation."

"Yes dear."

Betty and Linda Lou had dinner with the Montgomerys that night, and the next night too. Betty slept most of the next day. Linda Lou had totally charmed the folks and they were hesitant to let them go. After a week their friendship had strengthened. Both Henry and Miriam had asked them to stay on. Linda Lou loved to sit in the front window and watch the children pass by on their way to school. Miriam Montgomery suggested they might stay in town and even put Linda Lou in school. Betty felt exhausted even after a week of rest, and seriously considered the idea. Maybe it was time to put their Hollywood ideas on hold and get Linda Lou in school for a while. To find out more about the school, they walked there the next day. As they walked the several blocks toward the school, Betty noticed a For Rent sign on a tiny white house with a vine covered porch, and so it seemed the decision was made.

Chapter 19

MISS MIDSUMMER MILKMAID

RED BLUFF – 1959

The local milk company had put a tablet of applications on the counter in the restaurant where Betty worked. After reading it over a few times, she thought it would be a good idea to enter. She knew Linda Lou would have a good chance of winning the small town competition. After three years of lessons, she was a great little tap dancer. The show was in August when school was out. The prizes were one year of milk to the winner's doorstep, her picture on the milk cartons and a $100 US savings bond. Betty shopped every weekend for the perfect dress, finally finding it in a garage sale in the next city. It was hot pink with sparkles, a tulle skirt and lacy sleeves. It needed a little mending, but otherwise it was just what she needed. Betty had a great idea to glue pink sequins on her tap shoes. Linda would wear her pageant makeup of course, and her hair could be bleached. The winner was to ride in an open convertible during Hot August Days Parade. What a perfect time to take more photos for her book.

The trouble started as all the little girls were getting ready for the dress rehearsal in the bathroom of the Chamber of Commerce building where the show would be held. One little mousy brown haired girl went crying to her mother the minute she saw Linda Lou's new golden blonde locks, claiming that it was unfair. Another third grader quickly pointed out that the pink sequins were falling off the shoes all over the floor. The rehearsal was clumsy, with seven self-conscious girls not listening to the directions, and one professional trained in walking, turning, dancing and, most importantly, smiling straight at the judges. Betty was enormously proud of her daughter; sure she was going to win.

"Don't worry Linda, don't think about it. Remember what I've always told you. Someone is going to win and someone is going to lose. You just do your best."

The hall was full and chairs were scraping against the floor while a murmur of excited conversation was barely audible under the piano music of the grade school music teacher. Several of the girls were still dressing and Linda Lou could not find her sparkly pink tap shoes.

Linda's voice came faintly from behind the stall door, "Mom, where is my shoe box? Did you leave it in the car?"

"No dear, it's right there by your dress hanger."

"Mom, you put my dress on me...and the shoes are not here." They frantically searched the room, the floor along the hallway and then the car, but found no shoes. Linda Lou's face was beginning to cloud. "You forgot them! You forgot them."

"No, I wouldn't do that. Let me look in all the other stalls." With a quick look in the last stall, she discovered the box on top of the toilet tank, and the shoes deep in the water, sequins winking and floating. Betty was horrified that anyone would actually do this. Something had to be done and she made a quick decision.

"You will have to wear your street shoes. Hurry up, it will be just fine. I'll take ribbons from your hair and tie them to the straps. See, they look great. Let's get to the stage. It's even better if you are last. Just dance your regular steps and don't forget to smile at the judges."

She was last in line. The only girl in front of her was the baton twirler in a red, white and blue majorette costume. Poking Linda in the stomach with her baton, she hissed, cruelty peeking out from behind every freckle,

"You are NOT going to win."

Linda Lou looked beautiful. The audience oohed and aahed when she appeared. She danced as best she could, stumbling a few times. Her eyes kept darting to the side curtain to see the faces peeping out.

When the winner was announced, it wasn't Linda Lou. The brown haired girl who got the ribbon across her chest wore it with a smug smile. The fact that her father had worked at the milk company for eleven years wasn't even considered.

Chapter 20

FOURTH GRADERS ARE MEAN

RED BLUFF, CALIFORNIA – 1958

Bleached hair in the fourth grade wasn't normal. Boys would stare and follow Linda Lou. Girls would make fun, calling her hair a wig, sniffing, and declaring she was probably bald. All this happened the first week that Linda Lou was back in school. The more the boys looked at her, the more the girls ignored her. Linda told her mother when mean things started, someone pulled her hair, tripped her in the hallway, pushed her books off her desk in class, hid her coat, held her in the toilet stall and, finally, put a scrawled note on a paper plate in her locker, that said 'UGLY, UGLY, UGLY.' Linda Lou crumpled the paper plate, looking around to see who was watching. No eyes seemed to be looking directly at her, but she knew who had put it there. Tears sprang to her eyes as she rushed down the hall, running to Miriam's' where she went after school. She huddled in a corner of the couch and cried. After marching to the kitchen drawer, she took out the scissors, locked herself in the bathroom, and began hacking at her hair, tears flowing down her face. Miriam, of course, called her mother at work and she came right home. Linda Lou stood defiant in a circle of ragged, pale hair.

"I am NOT going back to that school. All the girls make fun of me and do bad things. Why do they? I don't want hair like this Mom, I want regular hair. I don't want to tap dance any more either. That's for babies."

Betty rubbed her head, looking at her daughter's tear stained face, then at the clumps of hair scattered on the floor. "I thought you liked to do the pageants. Remember, all our plans? You liked the blonde hair before when we did pageants."

Sniffing and serious Linda responded, "I don't care. I just want to be a normal girl with normal hair; and I want to take music lessons."

Sitting on the floor rocking her girl in her arms, Betty decided it was time to forget about the contests for a while. Linda Lou needed to go to school. They were in a good place for a few years. The answer was right in front of her. She would go to the drugstore, right then, buy a box of the new Miss Clairol Hair Color Bath, and darken Linda's hair, and maybe touch up some of her own roots. Linda would go to school, then to high school. After that they would surely get back into the pageant and modeling circuit. Her daughter would be grown and even more beautiful.

Then it would be time to head for Hollywood and make the rounds of the studios.

During the summer of Linda's eighth grade, Miriam fell and broke her hip and wasn't able to do after-school care for Linda. Betty looked for and found a larger rental just one block from the high school and that was their home during the next few years. Linda was selected to work in the school office after school and was able to do well there and complete her homework at the same time. But they still kept close to Henry and Miriam. Henry helped Linda Lou with her homework and Betty and Miriam cooked Sunday dinners together. Miriam passed away when Linda began her senior year and Henry was alone, and lonely. His brother, also a widower, offered him a room in his home in Leisure World, Seal Beach, California and he packed up his car saying to Betty,

"You are like my family, and I know that Miriam would want what I have decided. What do you think about moving into my house until Linda Lou graduates? Just take care of it for me until I put it up for sale."

Chapter 21

HIGH SCHOOL PROM

RED BLUFF, CALIFORNIA – 1968

Linda Lou flopped full length onto the sofa and groaned, "Mom, my high school prom is next weekend and I don't have a dress. We've looked everywhere at everything. They are frilly and babyish. I want something rad, Mom, really rad."

"What does that mean, 'rad? I never heard of such a word.

"It means – outstanding – stupendous, and radical."

Betty looked thoughtfully at her only child and replied, "I have one more place to look. Get ready for school and I will drop you off.' Betty drove from the school to the industrial part of town and parked in front of Harry's Costume Shop. The welcome sign in the window read "WE'VE GOT YOU COVERED". The bell over the door tinkled, and a tiny man with grey curls and many wrinkles stepped up behind the counter.

"I'm Harry. What can I do for you?"

Betty replied, "I'm looking for a pageant dress, size six or eight, something really outstanding." She followed the little man into a large, dusty warehouse that was crowded with racks and boxes of clothing.

"Just look through all these. Take your time, I've got all day."

Betty took out a pair of soft gloves from her purse and began shifting dresses, one after the other. The first one was black, the second low and strapless; she didn't like orange, so many were old and dated. She went to the second rack, bridal gown, too short, too long, wait – what is this? What size is this? Size eight, off one shoulder, slit up both sides, great for dancing. Betty held the dress up to the light, and it glittered blue and green in a material that imitated fish scales. Betty looked at the price tag and choked...but this was the dress. She made Harry an offer and after a minute or two of silence, he nodded and wrapped it up. Betty hurried home in high spirits. She knew she had THE dress. With a few blonde streaks in her hair and the dress Linda would be a knockout.

Linda Lou looked at the dress for a long time and then spoke quietly, "Mom it's beautiful. All sparkly and shiny. I love it. Herb will love it and the other girls will be incredibly jealous."

"You're going to the dance with Herbie Wong? That Chinese boy that works at the drugstore?"

"Only half Chinese, Mom. His mother is Spanish or Brazilian or something."

"What about that football player you dated a few times, didn't he ask you?"

"Yes, but I don't want to spend my prom night wrestling an overweight jerk in the back seat of a car. You know what they are all after on senior prom night. It's a dance, and Herb is the best dancer in school. He's a good friend, and it's sort of a going away date. He won a scholarship to a great college back east and his parents have already moved there and bought a house. He is the only boy in their family and he's going to be a pharmacist."

Betty looked away. "It's your night, honey." She knew at least there was no long term romance to worry about. They just had to get back into the pageant circuit, and this was just the dress that would get her back to it again. Graduation was next week, and then it would be time to start thinking about Hollywood. She had to get a copy of the Pageant News.

Chapter 22

RED BLUFF TO SAUSALITO

AFTER THE PROM, JUNE 1968

"Ready for another beer, Mike?" Betty's landlord had come to collect the rent as he did each month, and the stack of silver cans was mounting up in the trash bin.

"You bet, pretty lady. Are there any more chips?" Betty poured the last of the chips on a paper plate and took them to him with a cold can of Olympia beer.

"This is all the chips, only two more cans of beer. I've had enough. You should be going anyway. Linda will be home in an hour or so. I hope she had fun at the dance."

"An hour?" Mike looked hard at Betty. "That will just about give us time to kanoodle a little." Mike leaned over and gave her a wet kiss. "You're my girl, you know. My life was pretty dull before I bought this house from Mr. Montgomery and got you as a renter.

Come on; let's go in the bedroom where we can get comfortable."

It was a cloudless 2 a.m. when Herb walked Linda Lou to the door, giving her a hug and a friendly kiss goodbye. Betty was sound asleep, but Mike woke when he heard the door slam and Linda Lou walk to her room. He knew he had to get out of there or his wife would be pissed. Mike dressed and snuck into the living room and put on his shoes. The door to Linda Lou's bedroom was open and he could see her hanging up her prom dress, and stripping down to her panties and putting on her nightgown. His eyes fixed on her cute little ass and wondered if he could get some of that too. Mike moved soundlessly closer to the doorway as Linda got into bed reaching to turn out the light.

"Hey, Linda, you are a mighty pretty girl."

Drawing the covers up to her chin, her eyes wide, she asked, "What are you doing here? Get out of my room! I will call my Mother…Mom…MOTHER."

Mike sat on the edge of the bed, "Your Mother is sawing logs. I just want to talk to you some. Did you have fun at the dance? Did you let the guy get fresh and touch you here?" He rubbed his hand over her breast. "Did he get to first base? And how about second base?" Mike rolled his body part way over her; put one hand on her mouth, and the other fumbling under the covers near her nightgown. "Just don't make any noise and everything will be just fine."

Linda Lou thrashed and hit him with her hands, trying to scratch his face. She twisted under him; his body was large and heavy. His breath was sour and smelled of beer. She felt his fingers under her nightgown and frantically her hand slapped down on the nightstand onto her metal Disneyland bell. Linda Lou threw it with all her might out the door. It crashed and rolled, and the ringing woke Betty.

Hearing voices in the other bedroom, she hurried to the sound, saw the scuffle and saw in a horrific instant, the body of the man pinning her struggling daughter down. In a split second, and without thinking, Betty pulled the brass lamp from the nightstand and smashed it over Mike's head. He groaned and fell to the floor. Linda flew into her mother's arms crying, "Mom, Mom, what is he doing here? He grabbed me. Is he dead? What are we going to do?"

Hugging her crying girl, she soothed, "Are you hurt? Did he hurt you? Let me look at you. I'm sorry. He must have been waiting for you. No, he's not dead. Let me think. Go wash your face."

When Linda came back into the room, the lamp was back on the table, the bed was made and the window shade was pulled part way up. Betty said,

"I have a plan. Grab his other leg and we will pull him out to the front porch." Dragging him through the living room, one of his arms caught on a side table, and it teetered and almost fell. Betty dropped one leg and caught the table. After picking his leg up again, she pulled him to the front door, opened it and they bumped him over the doorframe, banging his head hard on the porch floor. Under her breath Betty muttered, "Serves you right, you schmuck." Pushing and shoving his bulky frame, they were both out of breath by the time he was finally settled in one corner of the porch.

"Now do as I say. Go in and make my bed and put out the ice cream with two dishes. I'll finish up out here." Betty grabbed a plastic lawn chair and an empty beer can, and racing around the house to Linda's bedroom. After dropping the beer can and propping the chair up against the side of the house, she stood on it to see what she could see in the room. Hurrying back to Mike's snoring figure, she unbuckled his belt and pulled down his pants. He was a jerk and a pervert and she was going to make him look like one. As she jerked on his pants, his wallet fell out. Thank you Lord, she thought. She decided to take back her rent; they were definitely not staying here. . Riffling through the bills, she counted out the rent which left him forty dollars. Then she hesitated, and then decided to take another twenty to pay for the lamp.

After locking the front door, Betty walked calmly to the telephone and phoned the police. Giving them her name and address, she pleaded, "Please come quickly, we have a Peeping Tom at our house that was looking in my young daughter's window. "I think he is drunk. Now he's on our porch."

Betty pulled out a pack of menthol cigarettes saying, "It looks like our decision to move on has been made. I will call into work tomorrow. We'll get a U-Haul and pack up. What do you think about heading for Hollywood?"

When the police arrived, they found a confused man, smelling of beer, with his pants down around his knees on the front porch and two women in their bathrobes eating ice cream in the kitchen.

The next day, Betty grinned as the car and U-Haul pulled away from the curb saying, "How would you like to have lunch at Fisherman's Wharf in San Francisco?"

"Great Mom, how far is it?"

"It's about two hundred miles. Get the map out of the glove box, you are my navigator."

Passing her school, Linda Lou waved goodbye to the school, the store, the movie house, crying,

"We are heading south!"

Linda dozed on and off during the ride and when she woke it was to a scene of white fluttering sails of boats dotting the blue waters of a beautiful bay. A packed marina with boats of all colors and sizes was snuggled up tight against the hillside.

"Look, Mom, boats! It's so pretty it hurts. It looks like a painting. Can we stop here?"

"No problem - I am ready. I have been following the signs to Sausalito Bay. Here we are; let's find a lunch counter." After eating a delicious hamburger and "the best French Fries in the World", Betty asked the clerk behind the counter,

"Any jobs around here? I'm a good waitress and a cook too."

"Not here, but I saw an ambulance leaving the Fish House about an hour ago. No one should be there but the owners and the cook. Maybe you should go see what's up?" The two walked the short block on a sturdy wooden sidewalk and looked appreciatively at the huge fish and chips sign – a picture of steaming golden brown fish slabs on a huge bed of curly fries wrapped in newspaper.

"There's no help wanted sign in the window, but let's go in anyway."

"WE'RE NOT OPEN," shouted the old woman sitting behind the cash register. "We might be closed today."

Betty flashed a quick smile, "We don't want to eat; I am just asking about a job."

The old woman threw her apron over her tear stained face, "My son, my son. He fell right there. It was his heart – just like his father." Wailing then, she rocked back and forth.

"Can I help? Can I get you a glass of water?" Betty hurried to the small gleaming kitchen and was welcomed by the aromatic smell of fresh bread that the cook was pulling out of the oven on long trays. "May I have a glass of water – for the lady?"

"Her name is Mrs. Nevins. Her son runs the restaurant. He is the one that just had the heart attack. They took him in the ambulance to the hospital, with his wife." Shaking his head, "If we don't open, lots of food is going to waste today."

Mrs. Nevins sipped at the water, "Thank you. What will I do? I don't know what to do. We are supposed to open in half an hour and I want to go to the hospital to be with my son." She was sobbing harder now. "I don't drive; can you call me a taxi?" Betty had been looking around at the pleasant little restaurant counting twelve tables covered with bright blue and white checkered cloths. Salt, pepper and malt vinegar were placed in exactly the same spot on each table. Her eyes strayed past the double doors leading to a small outside deck with painted picnic tables framing a wide view of the frothy bay and crowded marina. She looked at her daughter, who was nodding her head vigorously up and down.

"Mrs. Nevins, you don't know me, but my name is Betty Campbell, this is my daughter, Linda. I have been a waitress for twenty years, and I am a good one. If you trust me to work here, my daughter can drive you to the hospital. I will open up and work until you get back."

Mrs. Nevins stopped crying, and sniffed, looking intently at Betty, "You'd do that?"

Betty untied the apron and put it on herself, "We just need to walk to the car and unhook the U-Haul. We have only been in in town about an hour."

Mrs. Nevins beamed, "You are hired. You are both hired! Tell the cook."

"My son will not be able to work for a month or more", Mrs. Nevins announced when she returned that evening. "My cook tells me you are a good worker. I really need someone right now and I could use you. Can you stay for a while and help out?"

"I'd love to, but we need to find a place to live, right now, at least for tonight. We are both tired. Do you know of a place that we could rent around here?"

Mrs. Nevins shook a set of keys. "My son's wife wondered about that. Since they will not be using our boat at the Marina while my son is sick, she said it might work out if you and your daughter were to stay there until you found a place. Here are the keys, one for the gangplank gate and one to get into the boat. The walkway is right next to us. You can find it; it's called 'My Little Angel'…and that is what you are."

Betty and Linda snuggled under the light covers on the twin bunks. Betty was so tired; she didn't even take off her clothes.

"Mom, this is so cool. I can't believe it's real. It's just like a story in a book." The breeze was fresh with a tang of sea and fish. The continual rhythm of waves slapping against the side of the boat rocked her.

"I'm glad I'm in it, glad I'm…" and soon she was fast asleep.

For the first three months of the summer, Betty and Linda Lou were able to live on the boat. The neighbors on the dock became like family to them. . Robert, a retired banker and his wife, Rachel were on one side, with their boat named 'Bob and Ray', and two attractive men docked on the other side with their boat named 'The Dynamic Duo'.

Linda found a tiny apartment facing the bridge and the bay, up on the hill behind the hamburger counter where she helped out part time. Linda begged, "Just look at it Mom, you will fall in love." Grudgingly, Betty trudged up the two narrow flights of hillside stairs. "See - both rooms face the bay, and it has a cute little kitchen area."

Betty agreed, "That's just it, it only has two rooms."

"But they are BIG rooms," Linda pleaded. "You take the bedroom next to the bathroom and I'll sleep on the couch, it folds out. . . If I keep working we can afford it. Please, Mom. Let's look at the Pageant News. Maybe we can find something around here and I'll do a pageant."

Betty admitted, "It does have a terrific view, and we could sit out on the porch." She was secretly delighted that taking the apartment might lead them back on their way.

Linda won the Sausalito Bay Boat Queen Pageant, the Oakland Bay Bridge Top Model and the Carnation Milk Best in Show, which put her picture on a billboard. She won or placed in almost everything they entered for those years, which brought in a good amount of money and a scholarship at the local community college. The one she liked best was six months at a modeling school which included stage presence lessons and a personal pageant coach.

Then Betty Campbell fell from the deck of The Fish House and broke her ribs.

It was a Saturday and all the tables in The Fish House were full for lunch. People were standing in the foyer, waiting patiently. In the years Betty had worked there, she had come to know everyone by name and by boat. Mr. Nevins, the owner, only came in on weekends when they were busy.

"Does anyone want takeout?" Betty called.

One answer came from Spencer, who had a renovated PT boat. "Give me two to go and I'll be happy. I'll be outside on the stairs having a smoke."

Betty took receipts and cash from two groups at the cash register and turned quickly to the high kitchen pass-through when the 'Order up' announcement came. She shook her head as her eyes seemed to blur. She went to the deck and called to Spencer, "Here is your lunch, sweetie."

A wave of dizziness came over her as she leaned against the railing, hands out with an order in each hand. Suddenly, the railing parted from the corner post; she lost her balance and fell forward. One arm caught the edge of the stairway, and she hit it hard, rolling down the wooden walkway crying out, and moaning with each turn as parts of her body slammed into one unyielding step after another. Her head hit the metal post of the gangplank door with a dull thud, and then she lay completely still.

The patrons were all still, stunned by the freakish accident. Then the shouts started, "Stay off the deck. Get an ambulance! Is she dead?"

Mr. Nevins, the owner, hurried down to the crumpled figure. "Betty, Betty, can you hear me?" No answer. He picked up her hand and felt a solid pulse. "She's not dead, just out cold. Did someone call that ambulance?"

Out on the "Dynamic Duo", a short lunch cruise was ending, and Ronald and Steve were treating Linda Lou. They all heard the ambulance siren wail as they came into the marina.

"Thanks, guys, I really needed a break. I am so nervous about my big pageant tonight. What a way to relax." Waving goodbye, she hurried up the gangplank, then up two more flights to the small apartment. After showering and dressing, she checked her pageant bag carefully. Nick, her coach would be picking her up at the restaurant shortly. If she looked down, maybe she could see his car. Yes, he was there already talking to a group of people standing out in the street. She thought about Nick. He was a really sweet person, who had been good to her. She would be sorry when her lessons were over. She could tell he wanted something more. His friendly handshakes had turned into hugs and kisses, but business was business. She had ignored his increasing attention over the last months, but did appreciate how he had helped her. He seemed to be satisfied with a minimum pay daytime job at an exercise club but the truth was, she felt he was too old for her. She didn't want to be tied down.

The restaurant owner had been quick to tell Nick the news and he in turn had told Linda.. Linda Lou clutched her purse, white knuckled as Nick drove fast, but carefully, across the bridge to the hospital. Rushing to the desk in the lobby, she inquired about her mother.

"We have a Bet Camel in Room 206, right up those stairs."

Betty looked small and very white faced in the first bed, where a drip bag had been hooked to her right arm, and whispered,

"My eyes, my eyes went funny, got dizzy at the rail. Fell way down. Ache all over, head aches. Hurt-hurt," touching her chest.

Linda gripped her mother's hand, "Mom, I'm here, don't talk. Don't touch your bandage; you had a bad fall. Did you sprain your wrist? It's all wrapped. You rest and try to sleep. I'll be right here."

Struggling to speak, she replied, "No, No. You go…to pageant. Do it for me. Bring me crown. I will sleep. Love you to the moon." Betty's voice trailed off as her eyes closed.

Linda replied in their same old way, "Love you to the moon and back, Mom."

The nurse motioned for her to go now. She kissed her mother and was very quiet as she and Nick walked to the car. "I don't feel much like doing any pageant right now Nick, I'm sorry."

"Linda, this is the big one, "Queen of the Waves!" If you win in San Francisco at a regional, you go to State. You can't do anything for her if she is sleeping. Think of how happy she will be if you bring back that big diamond crown. We'll only be gone a few hours."

Back in the hospital three hours later, Linda hurried up the stairs to Room 206 with her pageant dress still on and a diamond tiara in her hand. The freshly made bed was empty and a small of disinfectant hung in the air. Wild-eyed, she ran to the nurse's desk, "Where is my mother?"

"She is in the recovery room, in critical care. Didn't she tell you she was going in for surgery?"

"No, she didn't. Where is that, where is she now?"

"Let me call the doctor, he will talk to you and take you there." The doctor walked along the hall with Linda and Nick, asking general questions about her health and if Betty was still smoking. "The fall is only part of her injuries. Your mother had a stroke that caused her to fall, and had another in surgery while they were setting her broken ribs. I am afraid she is sedated and can't talk right now."

Linda spoke quietly, "She will be all right, won't she? You can fix it. Just let me see her." The doctor laid his hand on her arm. "Well, you can see her for a minute; but just remember that some things are out of our control."

Linda Lou laid the sparkling diamond tiara on the pillow next to her mother's grey face and smoothed her hair back. Holding back tears, Linda whispered, "You need a perm, Mom. I'll bring your brush and makeup for you. Sleep and get better. I'll be right outside."

The doctor looked over the chart at the foot of the bed, saying, "She'll be sleeping for some time. You might as well go home."

Firmly, Linda answered, "Nick, will you get my bag from the car? I'm going to change my clothes, but I'm not leaving. You don't have to stay."

It was 3 a.m.; both Nick and Linda were dozing in the waiting room. A nurse, with an intern a few steps behind, stood shaking Linda's arm, and handed her the phone. "The Doctor is not here, but he needs to speak with you."

Linda listened groggily to the low, calm voice of her doctor advising her that her mother had passed away quietly in her sleep a short time ago.

The wake was held at The Fish House the next Sunday afternoon. Practically everyone who had a boat in the marina was there to remember their favorite server, Betty Campbell and to talk to Linda.

There were a few tears, but mostly smiles, laughter, and good stories. The fish and chips were on the house. Linda Lou hugged the owners of the restaurant, "Thanks for everything, Mr. and Mrs. Nevins. You have been so good to us. I am so grateful that you paid the hospital bill; Mother would have loved this party". Struggling with tears, "I will miss you."

"We will miss you too; you are welcome here anytime. You are probably welcome on any boat in the marina. Have you decided what you are going to do?"

"I have to go to the apartment and pack up everything. Nick asked me to visit him for a week or two to just sit by the ocean and relax. He has a two bedroom apartment right on Malibu Beach. I'm thinking about that." As the gathering was winding down, no one noticed Robert and Rachel, or Ronald and Steve leaving. The four of them went up the narrow stairs to the tiny apartment, and packed up Betty and

Linda's things in suitcases, and several cardboard boxes. They tidied up the two rooms, and, on top of one suitcase, left a white envelope stuffed with cash collected at the restaurant.

Streaks of pale yellow and pink coiled across the evening sky as Nick and Linda stood at the bottom of the stairway to her apartment, "Nick, I can't go up there."

Taking her arm, he said, "Let me help you."

"No, I mean I can't sleep there, not even one night. I can't be there in the middle of her things. Everywhere I look I will see her. What am I supposed to do?" She sat down heavily on the bottom step.

Nick sat beside her and laid his arm clumsily across her shoulders. "Let's worry about that tomorrow. Come with me tonight to the hotel. I'll get you a room." "I'd rather not be alone tonight. I'm not used to being alone. It's going to be dark soon; can I go with you and just be with you? I need to talk to someone. I just need somebody with me right now."

Nick looked thoughtfully at Linda, "Why don't we just pack some things and drive to my place at the beach."

In the apartment they saw that all the work had been done for her. Linda's eyes moistened when she picked up the envelope and the money. Heading for the cupboard, she found the oatmeal box her mother had always used to save the rent money. Without speaking, took it down and put the money inside, holding it tightly, and said quietly, "I'm ready now."

Chapter 23

MALIBU BEACH – 1972

Nick's apartment was the second floor of a big square house facing the ocean newly painted tan with bright blue shutters, and located next to a wide expanse of sand called Bonanza Beach. Someone else rented the first floor. Both apartments had large balconies hanging out over the beach with a 180 degree view of the frothy waves topping a constant blue ocean. Each day the sunny view was filled with oiled sunbathers, umbrellas, towels and kids screaming and splashing. Nick carried her suitcases and boxes into his guest room, saying,

"This is your room, just yours. I want you to feel safe. Don't worry, if the door is shut, I will knock."

The next morning they sat together on the balcony of his apartment, watching the sun rise above the blue green waves, steadily rolling onto the sand in their own subtle pattern.

Linda raised her swollen face to Nick and said, "Thanks for the orange juice. What would I have done if you hadn't been there? This happened so fast. I don't think I can do this by myself. She was the other half of me, more than half. She was the push all these years. She set up everything, she made all the arrangements, my hair appointments, and she did my clothes. Everything. There's nothing without her. It's over, it's all over. You don't know how that feels." Choking back her grief, she went inside and sat on the edge of the bed.

Nick sat next to her, smoothing her hair, "We can work something out. It's not over."

Taking a deep breath, his mind raced over what he was about to say. "What if I could be your other half, the two of us? Take me up on my offer, stay here at the beach and rest. Lie in the sun while I go to work at the exercise club. We'll just go on from here. You and me, Nick and Linda. What do you think? After kissing her forehead, he continued, "Don't cry, lie back and rest a little."

The first two days Linda Lou just sat in her mother's robe on the balcony and watched. On the third day, she took her towel and a lunch and went to the beach. For the next three weeks, she went to the beach every day, enjoying it, but speaking to no one. One Saturday, she laid her towel next to a couple who happened to be the neighbors below.

"Nick, the neighbors downstairs invited us to a barbeque. Do you want to go?"

"You bet I do. They make the best screwdrivers on the planet. Did they say to bring our own steaks? That's usually the deal."

Linda had her first screwdriver, then her second. The steaks were done just right, and the conversation was easy. The next day she had her first hangover. Cringing, watching Nick mix up a beer and a tomato juice to take out to the balcony that evening, she shook her head,

"That stuff isn't worth it to me, if you feel terrible the next day."

"Hair of the dog sweetheart, this and vitamin B. Come sit with me. I want to talk to you seriously. Are you happy here?"

Linda was slow to answer, "I love it here. It is just like a vacation every day. Look at that ocean, the beach. There are even trees. The sky is always blue and there are white fluffy clouds all over, so pretty. Did I ever tell you I see pictures in clouds? I think I see a whale up there right now."

Nick grinned, "You might even see a movie star or two. A few live up the hill. They filmed a movie here last year, right there on the sand on Bonanza Beach. You know, you should watch the Malibu Times for casting calls. What I'm getting at is this; I saw a blurb in The Pageant News about a bathing suit contest and wondered if you want to get back into it and enter this one. It's at the Balboa Yacht Club, just a small local competition. It's called 'Balboa Barbie'. It has good money for first, second and even third. I will set it up and do everything, sign you up and put up the front fee. Do you want to make some money? You said you could do some modeling. Don't answer now, think it over. You can stay here as long as you want to, either way."

"I do need to make some money. What do you mean, either way?"

Nick took her face in his hands, "Either you sleep in your own room, or you sleep in mine...with me. You are my girl, you know, and I'm crazy nuts about you. I'd like you to decide, but I think it's time."

Linda looked into his broad, open face, his serious hazel eyes. This was the partner that was by her side when her mother died, the man who had helped her, who had taken her to live with him. She saw the caring man who was to be her other half. She said quietly, "I've decided; help me move my things."

Chapter 24

SUNDAY BRUNCH, AN HOUR LATER - 1980

MISS MOCHA JAVA

No one noticed Fernando bring the third pitcher as they all were captivated by Linda's stories; Fernando never took his eyes from Linda's face as she spoke.

"It all went upside-down because of Miss Mocha Java. It was a contest in Redondo Beach, that's in California. I was living there with my manager, what's his name, Nicky. So there was this show he got for me, put on by a coffee company, and the winner would be their model for billboards and magazines. It was big pay. You had to be tan, of course, so I went to the beash, I mean beach, some days and laid out in the sun on our the balcony too. I worked on it for a long time… weeks, you know, putting that smelly baby oil and iodine mix on me, and I was tan almost all over, except a little sliver – you know where. She giggled and drained her glass, "I looked good, really tan." She poured the tall glass half-full and drank deeply.

"So, we girls all get ready to go out on the stage, but where is my manager? And where is the contestant from Puerto Rico? I called, but he didn't answer so I ran back to my dressing room… no one there, and on the way back I heard this sound from this broom closet so…I opened the door." Linda started to sob. "There they were, touching each other, you know where! Her bathing suit top was down and she had huge bosoms and I could see I was going to lose the contest; she was already very dark brown." She was wailing now. "She was buh- buh- buh brown all over! She was born brown, and she was rubbing on his privates."

Taking a breath, she rolled some beans in a tortilla and took a bite. Half of the beans fell out the back of the rolled tortilla and dropped onto her chest and tube top. One bean slid down slowly over the curve in between her breasts out of sight.

As Fernando picked up the plates, his eyes were glued to the trail of the bean, he thought, oh, lucky bean.

Bernie looked anxiously over at Linda not sure what to say, "Now, now, you are here with us. You need to forget about the things that make you cry. Hope you don' mind me asking you this queshun. How do you keep your hair up so high with so many curls, honey?"

"Oh, that's easy – look!" She pulled the curly piece straight up and off and laid it on the table, one curl landing in the guacamole dip. "I buy my curls; I have lots of them for the shows. I just wear a ponytail. Anyway, I just left him, then and there! It was over! I went home, packed my bags, took a taxi to the airport, and got here. Aw, look at my new blouse. What am I going to do?"

Juana spoke a few soft words in Spanish to Fernando and he nodded. "Go with Fernando and he will give you a clean shirt. It will wash."

Linda looked under the table, "I can't find my shoes." Bernie's eyes were closed. She was blissfully enjoying her second piece of double chocolate fudge cake with walnut frosting, reached down into her big woven purse and pulled out a pair of worn black ballet slippers. "Here try these."

Linda followed Fernando in the kitchen, took the shirt, and after thanking him with a wide drunken smile, disappeared into the ladies room weaving from side to side. . A short time later, a transformed Linda emerged. Her face was scrubbed clean and glowing. Her blonde hair was combed back in a small wave and ended in the back with a tiny pony-tail. A handful of freckles dotted her nose and cheeks. The oversize white T-shirt she was wearing only complimented her small breasts. Other than that, she looked like a very young girl. Fernando was staring unashamedly. Draping her arms over Bernie's shoulders from behind, almost falling on her she said,

"Thank you for the shoes; can I keep wearing them? You are so nice. You are both so nice. What does anybody do here? What do you do here, Bernie?"

Bernie handed a worn newspaper clipping to Linda. "I worked as a cook and companion when I first came here. I worked for Mr. Walters for years and one day he asked me to marry him. It was pretty much a surprise to me. This was about our wedding."

STARTING THE YEAR OFF RIGHT

Colonel Harlan Walters and Bernice Davis were married on the patio of his hillside home just before sunset on January 1st. The groom wore a white suit and the bride a powder blue dress that matched her eyes. The bride wore a corsage of white rosebuds and baby orchids. A dozen friends and neighbors attended the ceremony and afterwards all enjoyed a delicious prime rib buffet dinner with all the trimmings, champagne and margueritas, catered by the Gallo Loco. As if it were ordered, the blue sky, white clouds and one of the most dazzling sunsets of the year were a beautiful background for this event. The bride and groom were toasted with champagne. Violin music was provided by Fernando Alvarez."

Bernie wiped her eyes, saying "I remember it so well. They didn't mention that the groom was almost eighty years old. When it came time for him to say 'I do', he said, 'I do, because she fills my heart.' Now that's a memory. Been a lot of places and seen a lot of things. I married a soldier once because we were lonely; we both knew it wouldn't work. I had my share of men friends and Walter was my friend. I worked for him all those years but never slept with him. Maybe I should have. He was the nicest man I ever knew." Bernice closed her eyes and thought back to that day. "After the ceremony, he took my arm and walked me to the rail of the veranda. We set our champagne glasses on the ledge and looked at the incredible view. The sky was amazing, burnt orange, crimson and pink reflected in the water of the lake. There were even two white doves flying over. He looked at me and asked me how I liked being Mrs. Walters. I said I'd only been Mrs. Walters for five minutes and so far it was very nice. I liked the words the pastor said – 'I give you permission to disagree'. I never heard that before in a wedding. So I asked him if he thought we would ever disagree. I remember what he said; he always said the right thing.

"I don't believe we will disagree, Bernice. I liked the part where the pastor said 'from this day forward. Then of course 'til death do us part'. I never realized the real meaning of those words until just now with you, Bernice. I don't really like champagne, do you?"

"We both poured our glasses over the bank and laughed. He told me the sunset was just for me, and thanked me for marrying him. Our wedding was a great moment for me. Life is full of great moments; you just have to know when they are. I remember one day in particular."

Dinner was over which was a treat of Thanksgiving leftovers. Harlan and Bernice lay back in the comfortable lounge chairs on their deck. Bernie sighed deeply, "I will never get tired of this view; the lake is always different, such a gorgeous creation."

Harlan opened his eyes, "Yep, that's why I bought this land and built this house. I feel sorry for people who have never seen it. No one really knows where the name came from; some say it's an old Indian name meaning wet place. Lake Chapala is just one of many lakes caused by earthquakes and volcanoes millions of years ago – this is all that is left."

"Harlan, you know so much – you should write for the paper. Do you want to take a nice walk to work off some of this dinner?"

"Not tonight, Bernie; actually I am feeling a little melancholy. I think I'll lie down and take a short nap. "

"Now what is the cause of that? Was it because all the pie was gone?"

Harlan looked at Bernice intently, "You know that big brown package I sent off to my son last week? I signed the farm over to him; sent him the deed, the bankbooks and whatever else I had here for the farm. I am not sorry; it was time to do it. I have been meaning to do it for years and now it's all done. It's not on my mind anymore. I told him in my letter that I had put the house here in your name."

Looking surprised, Bernie said, "You didn't have to do that, Harlan. We have only been married these few years. What will he think?"

"He won't think anything. The farm is worth ten times over what this house is, and he cares for you just as I do. He would never want to live here. I won't be around forever. More than that, you are my wife and my friend, and you love it here. Friends take care of friends.

Solemnly Bernie replied, "I don't want to think about us not being together. You are the best part of my life."

He reached out and took her hand, looking at at their joined hands, his gnarled and spotted. "Bernice, after I'm gone, every time you think about me, we will be together. Even if you can't see me, I will be with you. Yes, I was thinking about your apple pie."

"I thought so! Let me cut up some apples and make a pie with cheese crumbles in the crust. You are good man, Harlan Walker." She bent down and kissed his forehead. "You go lay down a bit and I'll wake you when the pie bird sings."

Bernice sighed, "The Colonel has been gone now for two years now and I don't mind saying, he was a comfort to me. I never slept in the same bed with him until that last night. He said he wanted me by his side and held my hand. I think somehow he knew. Maigret has been living in the casita for quite a few years now. She bakes there and sometimes in my kitchen. Even then, it gets lonesome in that big house. We always talked about turning it into a Bed and Breakfast."

Juana folded her napkin and left the table in answer to the waving hands of friends and began to make the circuit of diners.

Maigret pushed her dishes to the center of the table and picked up her purse. "I can't eat another bite. Can I give you a ride home Bernie?"

Bernie answered, "Thanks, yes. It's time. Why did I eat that last piece of cake? Linda, will we see you here next Sunday?"

Linda grinned, "Oh for sure. This has been a wonderful day. I am so glad to meet you both. You are just what I needed. My head is spinning a little and I need my pillow for a while. See you next Sunday."

Chapter 25

SUNDAY, THE NEXT WEEK

IN THE COURTYARD- 1980

Linda was already at the table when Bernice and Maigret arrived. She had been to the buffet for fruit and cheese.

"Hello again. So glad to see you. I thought about you a lot this week. I started with a little fruit."

Bernie and Maigret took their usual places and Fernando brought the icy pitcher of margaritas and three glasses. There was a new dish today, Sausage and eggs on English muffins topped with sour cream and shredded cheese and Bernie took a double helping. Maigret ordered a strawberry waffle and Linda's smile broadened as she poured everyone a tasty pink margarita to enjoy along with their brunch.

Linda Lou slept on the table with one elbow in her half-eaten dessert plate, and her bedraggled fake curls perched saucily on top of a salsa bottle. Bernie was dozing on and off, head nodding after four trips to the ample buffet.

Linda raised her head, her eyes still closed, "I need to ask…are there any good men? I want to find a nice man – for me…before it's too late."

Maigret was collecting dirty dishes and stacking them to the side of her, "Of course there are good men. They are everywhere. It just depends on how good you want them to be. What kind of a man are you looking for?"

After breathing a deep sigh, Linda replied slowly, "I want a tall man, somebody that can dance. He has to be nice to look at, and not fat. He has to have a job to support me, and he has to love me, just me. I haven't had much luck with men. Who knows if I will ever find anyone? What if I don't? I am all done with this beauty stuff. I've got to find a job."

Maigret nodded, "You will find someone when you are not looking."

Fernando was clearing the table next to them, nodded his head up and down in agreement, wishing she would just look at him and thinking…look over here - he was tall and he could dance.

Bernice opened her eyes and coughed, "I heard that…I found a good man, the best ever. I wasn't looking; it just kind of happened. We weren't young either. You've got a lot of years ahead."

Linda lifted her chin, "The whole setup is kind of funny, isn't it? Women are nice and neat but men's bodies are so – untidy. Nick wasn't so good looking without his clothes. He snored...and worse. He even took baths! Have you ever heard of a man who liked to get into a bathtub? I guess he tried to be good to me though when I was with him. I was a model for Sears' catalog for four years and he got that for me. After a couple of years I went back to my own room and in a couple of years more, I knew that he was coaching and probably dating other girls. Still, to catch him flat out in front of me in a closet, well, that was just too much. That was the end. What is another word for privates?"

Maigret giggled, answering, "My little brothers used to call theirs weenies."

Bernice chimed in, "Well, on the farm when my brothers were all slicked up and going to Saturday night Grange dances, my father would say, 'Keep your willies in your pants, boys.' "

Linda laughed, "I like that better than calling it a peter. Imagine a mother naming her son with words for a man's private parts. I'll never understand that."

Maigret opened her mouth to speak, and a tiny margarita flavored burp came out. She started to giggle, and then Linda began to laugh, and even Bernice with her head down on the table chuckled. Soon they were all laughing.

Fernando stood frozen in place with his back to their table, his breathing short and choppy. Juana frowned at Fernando, but he did not notice. Her sharp mother's eyes had followed her son's lingering glances at the pretty blond.

"Fernando, clear the table, please." Fernando moved at a snail's pace, piling dirty dishes on a tray, stealing glances at Linda.

Juana looked intently at Fernando, "Clean the other tables as well, por favor; then go ask Carmen what you can do for her inside. Fill the wood box."

Heaving the wood pieces into the box with a heavy thunk, Fernando raised his voice and said, "Carmen, I am done here, I might as well go home". After glaring into the wood box, his eyes raised to the small violin that hung directly above it: his first violin. The idea came, and then a wide grin. He took it down, tightened the strings and tuned them, drawing the small bow across the strings, playing the beginners exercise A- A-E-E, "Twinkle, Twinkle, Little Star"

He stood in the doorway of the restaurant and began to play, swaying slightly, softly at first. When the diners noticed, he walked first to one table, then to another, playing one song after another. Standing behind Bernice, he played "I Love You Truly" as he had at her wedding. Walking past Maigret, he played "Little Boy Blue", then standing behind Linda Lou; he played "Little Gypsy Sweetheart" with his eyes closed and fingers skimming along the strings. Bowing to the applause, he asked, "Does anyone have a special request?"

Bernice cleared her throat and answered softly, "Do you know Clair de Lune?"

"Oh yes, it's one of my favorites. It's an old French song." He stood next to her, but looked across the table, rocking back and forth playing with extreme concentration, his eyes fixed on Linda Lou's rapt face. Bernice looked off in the distance, nodding her head to the music.

When he finished, Juana stood abruptly and thanked him. During the burst of applause, he started for the door enthusiastically playing "Guadalajara". As he reached the big barn door, a violin string broke. Holding the little violin up above his head, he bowed to the applause, smiling right at Linda.

Clapping wildly, Linda spoke, "How wonderful. I didn't know he could play the violin. It gives me chicken skin, I mean goose bumps."

Her eyes bright, Bernice wiped away a tear, "Yes, he played for my wedding. He was only about nineteen then. He is our local musician...the best." Wiping her mouth, and pulling her large bag to her hip, Bernice announced, "I have a plan. Maigret, let's all get in your little red wagon and go to our house. I picked up my mail yesterday at the post office and got a letter from the states. There is something in it for you. I can show Linda my house. We'll talk and Maigret can bring you back, Linda. You might think about helping me. I could use a house cleaner a couple days a week and you could keep me company in that big house. There are rooms there I haven't even used."

Maigret clapped her hands at once, "That's a good plan. I'll bring the car around."

Linda hopped up and hugged Bernice. "Oh, thank you, thank you. This has been the greatest day."

Bernice stood balancing herself against the table. "That's it, I'm all done. Let's pay our bill and go. I think I've had tee many margarooties."

Maigret, wearing Linda's red open toed shoes, walked toward the parking lot. A tall, distinguished looking man stopped her. He had seen the customer pick up the birthday cake and pay Maigret. Bernie couldn't help overhearing him introduce himself as Russell and tell her that he was impressed with her cakes. He mentioned that he was having a going away party for his brother the following Friday. He told Maigret he had invited a group of friends and was hoping that she could bring cakes, or, better yet, would she come to his house on the lake, make the cakes and stay for the party. Bernie smiled.

Chapter 26

LAKESIDE PARTY – 1980

The morning of the day of the party, Maigret followed the directions to Russell's home.

Her red station wagon was packed with pans and bowls, her mixer and utensils, flour, two kinds of sugars, milk cream, vanilla, and an apron.

"Hello, Russell; I found you."

"Yes, you did. Come in, and let me help you with those things."

An hour later, she had two long sheet cakes in the oven and was washing up and cleaning the counters. Russell had been out on the patio with his brother enjoying the lake view, but his eyes kept straying to the petite person in the apron in his kitchen.

"Come out Maigret, when you can. Sit for a while. Have some coffee with us."

"I will be there in a minute or two. Just putting my things back in the boxes."

Russell's brother greeted Maigret, shook hands and excused himself to finish packing for his departure the next day.

Maigret settled on a chair next to Russell, "I have about an hour to do nothing. What a wonderful view. You are very lucky. This is so peaceful."

Russell said, "It can get pretty rough when it storms, but even then it's a sight to see. I've been here for almost three years and never regretted buying this house."

Maigret sipped her coffee, "I'd love to live on the lake someday."

Russell answered cheerfully, "That could be arranged. Let me ask you this. Do you believe in love at first sight?"

Maigret lifted her head to look straight at him, "Did you just say what I thought you said?

"You heard me right."

"My answer is No, but I believe in like at first sight."

Russell grinned, "It's really not that far from like to love. Do you like me?"

Maigret set her cup down spilling some, "So your question is… do I like you? Like is such a simple word. You can like ice cream. You can like to take a walk. " She was quiet for a moment. "I guess I would have to say I do. So what?"

"You said you would love to live on the lake, and my brother is leaving tomorrow and giving up the extra bedroom. If you would love to live on the lake and you like me, we could try it and see where it goes."

Maigret stuttered, "But I have a business...I cook for a living. I'm not sure you would want me in your kitchen every day."

"Oh, but I would. I'm not here every day. I volunteer two days a week and go to class one day. I would like you here, just to be here. This isn't just a whim. I first noticed you last Christmas, there at the big brunch. I tried several times to get up the courage to speak to you. There is something about you that makes me feel good when I am with you. It just feels right. "

Shaking her head, "My rent is very small."

He took her hand, "There would be no rent, and no strings attached."

Cocking her head, she asked, "Is there a lock on the bedroom door?"

He flashed a big smile, "I'll put one there."

"I just can't up and move. I have cakes to make on Friday."

"You can use my oven. In fact, I could put in two ovens for you. I've already had a contractor here once about remodeling the kitchen and you could help me with that. Help me make it a kitchen fit for a cook."

The oven buzzer rang, and the sweet fragrant smell of baking drifted around them.
Russell followed her into the kitchen, bringing the coffee cups.

"So, what do you think? The lake and Russell - or Russell and the lake?"

Both were smiling as he leaned in to kiss her. He wrapped his arms around her, and the next kiss was serious. He kissed her slowly, open mouthed, and suddenly the night around them was electric. The feel of his mouth on hers created a bolt of energy that traveled through her shoulders and down to her fingers and toes.

He spoke urgently, impulsively, "Leave the boxes here. Come back to my house tomorrow, or just stay."

Pulling away, Maigret said quietly, "We need to talk. I'm not leaving anything here."

"Then come to dinner with me tomorrow night. Drive over and we will walk down the beach to a little French Restaurant I know. We can eat and talk."

"That sounds like a good idea. What time?"

Russell sighed a sigh of relief knowing he was going to see her again, "Whatever time you get hungry, or before."

That night the party was a gathering of about a dozen friends and neighbors; conversation came easy and most of the group moved from the finger food buffet to the patio, and soon everyone left . Some walked on the beach to their own homes. After the hugs and handshakes, Maigret and Russell cleaned up the kitchen quickly.

Back in her own casita, Maigret sat in her nightclothes on the patio talking out loud. "What have I got myself into? Did I find someone when I wasn't looking like Bernie said? We will see. He is really good looking, and easy to be with. I'm comfortable with him, but I am comfortable here too. Add everything up, him, the house and the lake. I guess I will know more tomorrow."

She remembered the letter Bernice had given her the day before. She picked it up and opened it to find a letter from her mother' in-law's sister, Janice Barnes. Scanning the letter quickly, she gasped, put it down, and then picked it up again. In part it read, "I am sending this through Bernice as I have her address on a Christmas card and I am not sure where you are. Many things have happened these past few months. Your mother-in-law, Barbara, has had a stroke and is in critical care. They called me as next of kin to come, so I took a week off my job and am doing what I can. Her stroke may have been caused by the arrival of two Navy officers at her door with news of her son's death and his personal effects. Jack had been living with a woman in San Diego and they had a child together. Unfortunately for all, the child, a girl, was born disabled and lived only three weeks. I must return to my job and my dogs in Northern California in a few days. Here is my telephone and address if you want to keep in touch. I went through her things and found these papers you might want.' Enclosed Maigret found Jack's birth certificate and a paid bill from an adoption attorney for a son to be named John Robert Stern and Jack's death certificate, with the notation of the cause of death as 'lost at sea'. There was also a slim envelope from the U.S. Department of Naval Affairs which she opened. In it was a letter that started, "We regret to inform you…" and a check for Jack's life insurance made out to her.

Maigret tossed and turned thinking about these events. She felt sorry for the poor child and the parents and hoped that Barbara would get better. She remembered a saying that her mother had told her, "When one door closes, another one opens," then finally relaxed and went to sleep.

The next night she dressed in her going to church clothes, took them off and chose a sleeveless blouse, slacks and a colorful striped shawl. Silver hoop earrings and a silver bracelet completed her casual look. She and Russell sat out on the restaurant patio holding hands, waiting for their dinner, watching the hypnotic rhythm of the dark waves, flowing repetitiously on the lake. The night was warm and dinner was flawless. By the second glass of white wine, somehow the conversation had altered from if she was going to move to when she was going to move. She felt the excitement in her grow like a rising bubble at the thought, conscious of the tall, attractive man holding her hands whose very presence made her happy.

She shook her head, "I can't stop smiling. I have to talk to Bernie and she will just say "I told you so." In a way, I hate to leave there. But she would want me to. Here's what I 'm thinking. I'll bake my goods early on Friday, deliver them...and go back to the casita and clean the kitchen, pack what I am going to bring and come here. Then I bake again on Sunday; because I always bake early Sunday. How does that sound?"

He squeezed her hands, studying her face, "No doubts, and no worries? I mean what I say, no strings attached."

"You won't mind a crazy kitchen every weekend?"

In a gentle tone, he answered, "I wouldn't mind anything, if I knew you were going to be there. After we clean up the kitchen on Sunday, we can take the rest of the day off." Russell had introduced Maigret to the owner, who recognized her name and asked if she might bake three dozen breakfast muffins for a men's club meeting he was having Saturday morning. He laid his arm around her shoulders as they walked down the beach, listening to the waves slapping onto the sand. They didn't talk much and when he asked if she wanted to come in for a while, she replied,

"I hope you don't mind, but I think I will stick to the plan. Thanks for the perfect night."

Chapter 27

THE HEART KNOWS

Fernando woke to the sound of turtledoves coo-cooing in the trees. He snuggled down under the covers to close his eyes again. He had been having a beautiful dream of riding a fine black horse with Linda Lou held snugly in his arms.

"Get up lazy bones. You need to open for me today," called his mother.

After showering and dressing quickly, always in his mind that he might see Linda Lou at the restaurant this morning, he raced through the kitchen. "No oatmeal Mama. I'll make coffee and have some fruit later."

Juana looked lovingly at her only child, now in college but still a baby in her eyes. "I must go pay Carmen for the week and have chocolate with her. You will need to take our money deposit to the bank."

"Yes, Mama', and I need to buy a thesis notebook for school."

Running down the hill in the half-light, he wondered in which room Linda Lou was staying.

Juana and Carmen sat in front of foamy, fragrant cups of chocolate as they had done every Monday morning for years. Living two doors apart, it was easy for them to have this time for woman –to- woman talk. Whether it was talk about their children at school, growing up, new clothes, or gossip about the neighbors or customers, this was their time. Carmen had been her stout support when her husband Hugo had died unexpectedly. Inquiring about Carmen's daughter, Marina and her beau, Miguel, Juana knew the conversation would drift around to what was really on her mind, which was Fernando – and his obvious infatuation with the blond 'gringa'.

"But Carmen, she is not for him! He does not listen to what I say. She is a foreigner and he is being foolish."

Carmen sipped her chocolate, "Maybe she will be gone soon."

"No, I don't think so. She is going up to the White House to live with Senora Walters. What can I do?"

"Juana, you can't tell the heart who to love. He is twenty four. Once the heart sees its first love, it is very hard to tear it away. It was that way for me when I first saw Manny. If I were you, I would do nothing. Just wait and see. Be like a rabbit in the grass. Watch and wait."

Fernando opened the restaurant, turned on the lights, made coffee and brought in the basket of fresh bolillos left by Rosa. Intentionally making noise by scraping chairs and tables across the flagstone patio, he kept glancing at the motel doors, to see if she had heard. Door three opened, and there she was, standing in the portico, dressed in blue, pale hair slicked back on each side with child's barrettes. Blinking his eyes to make sure that she was real, he stood still as she walked toward him.

"Good morning Fernando. It's nice to see you again. My name is Linda Lou Campbell, call me Linda. Do you think I could have some tea and toast?"

His lips seemed stiff, "Yes – no, I mean, I have fresh coffee and rolls."

"Oh, that's fine. I take lots of cream in my coffee. Can you sit with me? Talk to me, and tell me things about this place."

He sat, and they talked and smiled and looked into each other's eyes. To him she was something entirely new. She had a perfectly shaped nose below thick dark eyelashes around clear grey eyes. The light provided a shine to her golden hair. He could have looked at her for an hour without speaking especially her perfectly shaped lips. But all he could say and then with a stutter was that she had nice hands. He could not remember what they talked about, except that she did say she was moving to Bernice's house that afternoon. Fernando was captivated. He had never met anyone like her. He looked at her slim fingers and hands curled on the table top. Inch by inch, his hand moved toward hers and touched one finger.

"You have pretty hands, long fingers. You could be a musician." Fernando heard his mother's truck coming down the hill and said quickly, "I have to go to the bank right now. Do you need to change your money to pesos? I will take you."

"I never thought of that, but I guess I do. I'll go get my purse."

"Go out to the front of the motel, to the road. I will pick you up."

After taking the dishes into the kitchen, Fernando took the keys and the money bag from his mother and drove out to the highway. Juana was banging pans and did not notice the sound of the truck stopping and starting.

They drove in silence for a while, Fernando watching her out of the corner of his eye.

"You are going to live at the White house?"

"Yes, I am so excited and lucky too. Fernando, you are really good on the violin."

"My father taught me. He played too. I started when I was four."

Linda pursed her lips, "I don't know whether to tell you or not, but I took violin lessons in school, fifth and sixth grade. I borrowed the violin from the music room. I should have stuck with it."

Fernando turned his head and looked squarely at Linda, "You really want to learn to play better?"

"Oh, yes."

Seeing a way to be with her more, he replied, "I could teach you; I could give you lessons. Here is the bank. After we finish we could go to the 'Mercado', the market in the plaza. Do you need anything?"

Clapping her hands, she nodded, "Yes, I do, I forgot lots of things, girl things."

Awed by the sights in the market, Linda stared open mouthed at the colorful piles of fruit, the hanging raw meats, dozens of white cheeses, and the fragrant masses of every color of flower. They stopped in front of huge rotating racks of appetizing roasting chickens, whose aroma seemed to follow them. She walked two times around the edges of all the market areas and delighted in all the new sights and colors. She made her way to the middle to the tables of cosmetics where she stopped and said, "I'll take this, and this ...and a banana and some grapes."

Fernando steered her out to the entryway, "Let's get some coffee and sit on a bench. I need to stop here to buy a notebook for school. I go to college in Guadalajara and stay there all week and come home on the weekends. But I could come to your house and teach you on Saturdays in the afternoon, after I finish teaching Ruby."

"I guess that would be all right. What are you taking in school?"

He answered, "I am in my second year of business and hotel management. I am leaving for school as soon as I drop you off at the motel. I will see you next Saturday. "

Chapter 28

TWINKLE, TWINKLE, LITTLE STAR

Three weeks after they first met was the day of the first violin lesson. It was hard to say who was more nervous: the student who would have to play in front of the teacher or the teacher who could easily pass on his knowledge but knew that the reasons for wanting to spend time with Linda were more than musical. The lesson was to be upstairs in the common room. Fernando handed her his small violin, "First, let's go over the names of the parts of the violin, this is very easy. Show me how you hold it. Good, that's very important. Do you know the names of the strings? G – D – A – E. Can you read sheet music?"

Linda admitted, "A little, if it is very easy. I know some of the scales but it's been a long time."

Fernando raised his eyebrows, "Good. Let's do one scale. Close your eyes and just listen to it the first time. This is 'A'. Let's play it together. Good. Now you play it alone. It will be slow at first. Soon you will play it forward and backward. Next week we will do another one. Do you remember anything by heart?"

Linda thought, "I think I can do 'Allouette' and 'Twinkle, Twinkle, Little Star."

Smiling, Fernando said, "Next week we will play them both. This week, just practice them and the scale. Now that wasn't so bad, was it? Be sure to put the violin and the bow in the case every time after you practice. I have to get back to the restaurant. See you next week about the same time."

The violin lessons continued all during the rainy season, for about four months. Linda finished Book One and Book Two and was easily learning and memorizing new songs from Book Three. Sometimes Fernando joined in as a duet. By then, the hello hug and goodbye kiss became longer and stronger. But just as wars are started with a small insult, the discovery of their secret began with a sniffle and a small sneeze.

Ruby was sick with a bad cold and she told Fernando the day before, that she was sick and hadn't practiced so there would be no lesson. Unfortunately, Carmen came down to the restaurant to tell Juana to tell Fernando not to come. But Fernando had already taken the truck and gone, saying he was going to Ruby's lesson and to get a haircut. After his lesson with Linda, they both went to the barber to get a haircut; her hair was growing out of the bleach into a darker blond. She had it cut short in a boy's haircut, and on her it looked adorable.

His mother asked how the lesson went with Ruby; Fernando lied, and said "same as usual'. Juana caught him in the lie, and he stammered a little but then had to admit he had been giving violin lessons to Linda for many months, explaining that she had some lessons before and was doing well as she worked her way through Book Three.

Juana didn't want to listen, and instead demanded that he quit seeing her, that he cut off the lessons and the friendship and work more in the restaurant so he could be a partner one day.

"Please, Mama, listen. I am twenty five years old and I will finish college in eighteen months. Please listen. I want you to see how I feel. I know that in your lifetime one perfect love comes, as it did with you and my father. One love as strong as iron. I cannot let this go. This is my chance, and I have chosen her. She wants to be with me in my future as well. When I finish college and if we marry, no, when we marry, she will need me with her. I have never felt this way about any girl, just her. I love you Mama, with all my heart, but don't you see? Be happy for me, Mama, for us." The truth was told and he smiled at his mother and felt relieved.

Juana looked down at her hands clasped in her lap. Her son had given her so much joy all of his life. He was a Christmas gift to her from his father and there had been no other children. There had just been the two of them since his father died fifteen years ago and this is how she had hoped it would stay. "You are all I have and you will be leaving me."

Fernando put his arm around her shoulders and hugged her to him, "What is a son without his mother? Mama, you are my wings. You taught me to fly. Do you see the future? I do. You are in the middle of it. I am not leaving you, she is coming to us. Then there will be three of us as a family. Remember what you used to say to me when I was a boy, 'go to sleep happy'? Go to sleep happy 'mi mamacita'. We need you in our lives - you are part of our plans. Do this for me, go to sleep happy. "

Chapter 29

THE RECITAL

IN THE COURTYARD – NOVEMBER – 1980

The day selected for the recital was the third Monday in November. Ruby was bursting to show off what she had learned. Linda was almost finished with Book Three, and, thanks to her perfect memory, was easily learning and memorizing new songs for the recital.

The day coincided with the holiday of "Dia de la Revolucion" and a large group was coming for lunch to the restaurant and the tables would be filled for the political speeches and then the recital.

Ruby was first to play, performing 'Michael Rowed the Boat Ashore', and then the 'Soldiers March'. Linda played next, 'The Impossible Dream'. Then Linda and Fernando played a duet, 'Noche de Malaga'. Fernando called Ruby up and the three of them played a bouncy variation of Twinkle, Twinkle, Little Star" that had the crowd clapping and smiling.

As a solo Fernando performed 'Mi Estoy Enamorando' (My love is Here) swaying and stepping back and forth. Linda stepped up next to him and played 'Solomenta Una Vez '(You Belong to my Heart) Then Fernando began to play 'Promesa' (The Promise) on his knees before Linda. It was when Linda went down on her knees facing him, playing just to him, that the audience realized it was more than just a recital and sang along with the words, "I am on my knees before God to let me live longer so I can love you longer" and when they smoothly swept into 'Amor Eterno' everyone began to stand and clap and shout, including Bernie and Maigret. After ending with a flourish and oblivious to anyone else, Fernando kissed Linda gently. Fernando finished the recital walking in between tables with a rousing version of the National Mexican Hymn.

Juana, who had been standing in the doorway watching, and gripping her apron, glared at her son as he went by, and turned away from him back into the restaurant. She sat heavily onto the wooden kitchen chair with her head in her hands. She thought back to her life and the path that had brought her there. She closed her eyes and felt like she was floating and saw herself as a child.

JUANA

Chapter 30

JUANA REMEMBERS

GOING TO THE WEDDING

Juana was almost five years old, happy and dirty playing in the mud puddle outside of her parents' small rented house. Hearing her mother call, she got up slowly, squishing her toes in the puddle one more time.

"Look at you! Nana is coming and you look like a beggar. She will have to give you a bath after we leave. I want you to be a good girl while Mama and Papa are gone on their trip. We are going to the bus station to get on a big bus. Eat your breakfast and go to bed when she tells you. She will sleep here and take good care of you. Do you remember how many days we will be gone? Count for me, Uno, Dos, Tres, Quatro, and Sinco. Sinco days. How many fingers is that?"

Juana could see her Papa loading their suitcase into the taxi and Nana walking up the street. Her face started to crumple. Her Papa grabbed her and lifted her over his head,

"Don't cry my Juanita. We are going to my brother's wedding in Patzquaro. We will bring you back a present." After putting her hand in the hand of Mariah, the competent woman who came to care for her, her parents got into the taxi and waved a smiling goodbye.

"We will be back soon."

They did not come back soon, not in five days, five weeks, or even ten weeks. Mariah's son-in-law wrote a letter to the brother in Patzquaro, who replied they had never arrived. They notified the police, but no one had seen them. When the property owner knocked on the door after the second month for the rent, Nana Mariah and her family had to make a decision. Mariah, her daughter and her daughter's husband, a lawyer, discussed the possibilities. There was only one conclusion. Juana would come to live with them in the casita with Mariah, who would care for her as she had always done as her Nana.

Moving day was solemn. Boxes were packed and important papers put away, except for the bankbook from Lloyd's bank. Mariah's son-in-law looked it over carefully, thinking of all the circumstances. After a sleepless night, he came up with the answer. As lawyer for both families, he felt it was their duty to care for Juana. He made a request to the court that Mariah could take out her wages each week from the Lloyds bank account of the parents. This took another two months to finalize. For many months after the move, Juana would go to the door and look out, counting to five.

Soon after the move she started school with Mariah's grandson, Marco. The three of them would have breakfast together and Mariah would walk them to school. Juana grew to love Marco as a brother. She thought of Nana Mariah as her grandmother. The years passed and the children grew as one family and no one remembered a time that Juana did not live there.

Juana was a good student, and through the years would help her 'brother' with his schoolwork. When she was ten, she began caring for the neighbor's children. When she was twelve, she got a job hanging up clothes in a second hand store. At fourteen, she was sweeping and stocking shelves at the grocery store, and at fifteen she was making beds at the Casa Redondo. At sixteen, along with her school friend, Carmen, she began helping the owners, Hugo Alvarez and his wife, at the El Gallo Loco restaurant after school, by bussing tables, washing dishes, working in the garden and the best part, gathering eggs.

Chapter 31

THE RESTAURANT

NEAR LAKE CHAPALA

Hugo had built the barbecue grill just inside the barn door when he first converted the weathered barn into a restaurant. Now it was used as an additional cooker for roasting, and to keep the coffee warm for the guests who might wander over from the motel across the courtyard for the coffee and rolls included with their room. The Gallo Loco (Crazy Rooster) was open for breakfast and lunch, and on Sunday, only for the Brunch. It was a small, friendly, family run loncheria with very good Mexican food. Many of the locals had been customers for years and it was a gathering place for meetings and parties.

Next door and sharing a circular driveway is the Casa Redondo, (Round House) that had been first remodeled by the parents of Dolores Diaz. They had gone to Hugo and his wife, a promising young couple and friends of their daughter, asking them if they would be interested in opening a restaurant in the barn building. With their financial help, he had worked hard and surpassed all their expectations. The barn became a restaurant and the stable became a busy motel of five rooms, once stable stall with doors of heavy oak, crisscrossed with metal strips. The wood doors felt sturdy and warm when one opened them. Chevron shaped red brick stones made a spacious walkway eight feet wide in front of and between the colonial arched porticos over each doorway. Dolores Diaz, now the owner, lived in Number One, and the storage room in Number Two was the old tack room. In it were the supplies, linens, pantry, washer and dryer, and yard care tools. The tack room had been shortened to make a tiny galley kitchen for the owner. The rooms opened onto a tranquil courtyard with a few tables and chairs. There was parking in front and a gravel road that continued in a semi-circle around a grassy area and eventually passed by trees and the outside seating area for the restaurant and then back out to the highway.

Hugo had remodeled the rustic barn building over time into a restaurant with a welcoming front door and windows, but had kept the big barn door at the side. The lofts of the barn were still in place and the high ceiling of warm honey colored wood reflected the lights from the hanging lamps over each of the eight tables. The barn door was now a large sliding door which opened to the flagstone patio facing the motel. On that side had been added several outside tables with white plastic chairs and a picnic table, shaded by a huge lacy jacaranda and two pale pink-blossomed trees high behind it. A dozen clay pots at the front and side door blazed with color and fragrant herbs. Growing absolutely out of control over part of the front door was a flowing, fire red bougainvillea, and next to it a huge lime tree, its laden branches touching the ground. Built along the back of the building, next to a high wall was a small fenced area with a rectangular row of boxes. There dusty white chickens, proudly laid a few eggs each day while the rooster, too wild to be penned up at night, slept in the trees, noisily welcoming each day.

Far back in the restaurant yard was a large fenced garden that Juana used daily, changing plantings according to the seasons. She had lettuce, strawberries, tomatoes, onions, green and red peppers and bushes of tiny, very hot peppers. Small yellow squash, carrots, cucumbers and potatoes flourished. Green beans climbed crazily to the top of the high back fence. All grew vigorously with the help of the daily restaurant scraps and an occasional infusion of goat manure. On the other side of the wall was a dead end street, and a large field of chayote, a bumpy green vegetable, cousin to squash, where the fruit grew down in a jumble from an overhead framework of wires and ropes. The road ended between the chayote field and the old blue house built by the parents of Dolores Diaz that was now rented to Rosa, the bolillo maker. From there was a weed and high grass bordered path to the beach and the edge of age old Lake Chapala. There was a time long ago, when the lake was the magnet of the town and every evening the entire village sauntered to the lake's edge to wash clothes and themselves.

Chapter 32

HUGO DECIDES

Gradually Hugo began to be more aware of Juana. He watched her confidence with the customers, serving food, cleaning up and taking the money. She smiled and talked easily as she worked, soothing babies, and giving special attention to the elderly, in good spirits all the time.

This day, a boisterous group of young farm workers were laughing and eating on the outside patio, each one slyly admiring Juana. One in particular asked Juana repeatedly to go to the lake with him. Finally, she tossed her head, put her hands on her hips, pointing to them one after the other,

"You are too tall, you are too short, you are too skinny, and you have no mustache!" During the loud laughter that followed, they did not see the dark looks sent their way by Hugo, who was trying not to listen.

Hugo looked around and saw her touch in everything: the new curtains at the window, the shining silverware, and the one real flower in the vase on each table. His eyes travelled back to Juana, and suddenly he did not see a smiling efficient server in an apron, but a very desirable woman. She was much more than just a dependable and hardworking part of the restaurant. He sat down slowly in a nearby chair overcome by the startling fact that he could not imagine how it would be without her.

Hugo watched Juana intently, cleaning the last of the day's dishes. Each time he looked at her, his feelings swelled. He realized that he wanted her for himself. Juana, with the radiant and generous smile, the huge brown eyes between thick black lashes, and the long, familiar braided hair. He wondered what her hair looked like loose and long. He thought of her soft breasts under her white starched blouse. His thoughts were those of a man reaching out to a woman; he began to harden and rise.

It had been two years since his chubby, dimpled wife had drowned in Lake Chapala. He had several unhappy months after she died. More than one time each week he would drink too much and at the end of the day would leave restaurant lights on and the doors open. Several times Dolores noticed the lights and found him asleep on the floor, turned off the lights, and closed the restaurant, leaving him there. After those dark months he returned to sound management at his restaurant, while at the same time he slowly worked on building his house on the lot given to him by his father.

In the last two years he realized how much he had become dependent on Juana. Juana opened the restaurant, collected the eggs, baked the sweet rolls each morning, tended the garden and, once in a while, cooked breakfast for the early risers that came in before Hugo arrived to cook. Now things had shifted and changed abruptly.

As they were preparing to close, Juana asked if she could leave early to shop for decorations for the next day's Valentine's Day lunch. Hugo turned away and said,

"Yes, go. I will close up."

The familiar melody of many tiny, unseen birds chirped merrily in the dark overhead, as Juana passed under the trees that lined the street. 'To-eat, to eat, too-too sweet.' This was to be a special day, a big day for the restaurant. She was arriving early to set up the tables, the pink hearts and red carnations she had bought at the ''tianguih', the street market, the prior day.

She stepped over the flagstone patio, unlocked the door and looked in amazement. There were pink and red hearts everywhere. They were on the walls, on the ceiling, on the tables and swinging from the lights.

She exclaimed, "Who did this? Hugo? He must have stayed very late."

In the kitchen, she removed her shawl, turned on the oven and began arranging the tables, four on the right side, four on the left and four outside the big barn door.

She was making frosted breads today for breakfast and jalapeno twisted biscuits to go with the roasted fish meal. She had made caramel flan the previous night. Singing softly, she mixed the flour, yeast, milk, sugar and eggs, kneading with her hands until the dough was shiny. After covering the bowl to let it rise, she went to the chicken corral to collect what eggs might be there. She was glad to hear Hugo's truck drive up. He came in carrying a brown bag with bottles clinking,

"Buena Dias, Juana. I brought something for the men today."

"Hugo – you did all this?"

Turning away from her, he said, "It was nothing. I had extra time last night and today is not just any day."

It was a good and special day. They worked side by side, preparing the scrambled egg and sausage breakfast with three salsas, cheese and mushroom enchiladas and roasted potatoes. Enticing smells of baking and coffee floated through the air. All went on the counter as a buffet with the sweet rolls, tortillas, coffee, iced tea and a huge platter of sliced fruit and cheese.

After the surge of breakfast customers, Hugo and Juana were in the kitchen again beginning lunch: chopping, slicing, and placing the fish filets in long pans, sprinkling them with chopped almonds and parsley, pouring a mix of butter and spices over them.

"More salsa Juana - I need more limes, check the outside tables, throw some crumbs to the corner so the sparrows will stay away from the tables." Smiling and good natured, Juana handled the customers, serving, clearing tables and helping in the kitchen. Then everyone was gone and there was no food left: no fish, no rolls, no dessert, nothing but a few vegetables.

Hugo motioned with his arm, "Come sit and rest. This day is over and you have worked hard. Have a drink with me." He took out the unopened bottle of Tequila and one of Kahlua.

"Oh no, Hugo, I am too tired, just a soda for me." She watched as he poured her soda and his Kahlua with a splash of tequila. They drank in silence.

Clearing his throat, he said, "I will drive you home tonight. Juana, how long have you worked for me?"

"Six years, Hugo, maybe seven. Is something wrong?" She sat up straight in her chair.

Hugo looked into her eyes for a long time and said, "I was just thinking that we work together well. Don't you think we are good together?"

Relieved, Juana answered, "Yes, I think we are."

Hugo poured another drink, this time with a larger splash of tequila. Taking a deep breath, he said slowly "I think we should be together, really together...all the time. I think it would be good if we got married."

"What?" Juana had an odd feeling, as if the table and his face were slipping far away into a very small circle and she was high above on the ceiling, looking down.

Hugo took her hands in his tightly, his face serious, "I – want you with me all the time, daytime and nighttime. I would like us to live together. I want to see you wake up beside me. Tell me, what do you think?"

Her eyes rose to the familiar, serious face of the man she had admired and worked side by side with these many years, then looked again at all the pink and red hearts.

She said, "I like the way you smile and laugh. I like the way you run the restaurant. You are a good cook and I love working here. I don't want to be anywhere else. Oh, that was not what I wanted to say. Yes, we are good together."

"Does that mean we will get married?"

"Yes, Hugo. Yes!"

He leaned over, kissed her saying, "Good. We will go to the church and talk to the priest."

Chapter 33

NANA MARIAH

Juana sat quietly as they drove through the warm night, but her thoughts were jumbled, flashing and darting with one repeating theme; *He wants me, he wants ME!* As they turned the corner towards the casita she shared with her adopted grandmother, they saw the doctor's black sedan in front of their gate. Behind the black car was a red and white ambulance.

"Oh no, something has happened!" she cried. Juana jumped out before the truck stopped. Pushing hard on the half-gate, she could see the ambulance drivers carrying Nana on a pallet across the courtyard into her daughter's house, the doctor walking next to her.

"What is it? What has happened? Is she all right? Are you all right, Nana?"

The doctor took her arm. "Mariah had a dizzy spell and fainted. Her grandson found her. She could have had a small stroke but nothing is broken. She is talking a little but doesn't want to go to the hospital, so we are putting her in the sunroom for now where her daughter will be able to care for her."

Wringing her hands, Juana spoke, "What can I do? I will stay home from work tomorrow. I can help."

The doctor put his arm around her and said, "Mariah has been coming to me for over a year now with problems. Her eyesight has been dimming and she has shortness of breath and headaches. She would not let me tell you, but this is no surprise to me. She will have the best of care with her family. Go in and talk with her. She is asking for you. The men are going to bring over her bed. I am glad Hugo is here to help."

Juana hurried to her Nana's side, noticing how tiny she seemed, this small grey-haired woman who had loved and cared for her for over fifteen years.

"Nana, I am here. You didn't tell me you were feeling bad or I would have stayed home and helped you more."

The answer came in a weak voice, "Don't worry about me. I have been thinking it is time I moved in with my daughter so you could have the casita for yourself. She is right here all the time working in her paper goods store in front and she can keep me company. You are a grown woman now and need your own home."

"Oh Nana, I have wonderful news. I am going to have my own home. Hugo and I are going to be married, and his house is almost finished."

"Juanita, my sweet girl, this is just what I have prayed for…that you would find a good man. I cry with happiness for you." Her voice was weakening. "Go to my dresser, and under the Bible is a package. There are things in it for you that were your mothers. Take whatever you wish from the house, the rocking chair, dishes, anything, and everything. I am tired now."
Her eyes closed and she slept.

Laying the Bible on top of the dresser, Juana pulled out the brown paper package tied with twine. Inside was a sepia photograph of her parents on their wedding day, a filmy floral head scarf that she could see her mother wearing in the photograph, and a pair of gold hoop earrings. In a wrinkled envelope was the black bankbook with "Operadora de Fondos Lloyd, SA" stamped on the front. Seeing it brought back the memory of their weekly bus rides to the cool and quiet bank in Chapala, standing in line to pick up the small amount of pesos allotted to Nana for her care. The nest egg her parents had started so many years ago was to be their gift. It had grown and grown. Looking at the book and reading the last balance, she could not believe her eyes when she saw that it was many thousands of pesos. Could it be right? She would go to the bank the next day.

Several weeks later Hugo and Juana were married quietly with Dolores Diaz and the priest as their witnesses.

That evening together in their home there was no uneasiness between them as they undressed to get ready for bed. Her hair was unbraided, long and wild curls rested on the embroidery of a simple white sleeveless nightdress.

Holding her away from him, he murmured, "My beautiful bride, what do you know of marriage and love between a man and woman?"

Juana touched him lightly on his arms, "I know what I have heard, but I do not know exactly. With you, I want to know it all. I know it will be right because we are together."

Chapter 34

THE GIFT

Christmas was just a few days away, and the restaurant daybook was filled with reservations and parties. The many business lunches, club lunches and families exchanging gifts had increased the holiday atmosphere. The room sparkled with decorations, and dozens of bright red poinsettias and many colorful packages were scattered under a huge green tree. The delicious smells of baking added to the anticipation. Juana and Hugo were eagerly awaiting their turn as the children's Christmas march, the 'Posada' was set to visit the next evening bringing many children to reenact the plight of Mary and Joseph seeking shelter. There would be dozens of girls dressed all in white, walking in front with Mary and Joseph on burros, and musicians walking behind them, not to mention the parents of most of the children. Every child would receive something from the business owner, such as candy or an orange.

Juana was finishing cleaning the kitchen as Hugo brought in all the chairs and locked both doors. "Juana, mi amor, I have something for you."

"One minute. I'm almost done. Let me put this basket of oranges by the door."

Taking off her apron, Juana walked toward Hugo where he sat in the kitchen on one of the wooden chairs.

"Did you buy a piñata? Where is my present? What have you got for me?"

"Yes, I bought two. Come sit on my lap first and I will show you." He lowered his trousers, drew her across him and kissed her soundly. His fingers traveled down the buttons of her blouse. "Let me see you," he whispered as he exposed a good expanse of creamy skin. His eyes rushed to the black velvety nipples turning up for his kiss. His fingers burrowed into her clothing and scratched lightly across the band of her panties.

"Let me in, mi Amor," he whispered. Juana felt the curl of pleasure start between her legs and closed her eyes.

He pulled her close and scattered light kisses over her face, pressing his hardness against her. Gruffly, he said,

"Raise your skirts, woman."

Juana straddled his lap and he moved aside the scrap of material under her clothes. She stood up slightly and then lowered herself onto him slowly, leaning back so he could see himself disappear in her. Hugo groaned, ripping the shred of cloth that separated them. She raised and lowered herself on him, almost pulling out each time, and finding a rhythm until her thighs were quivering.

Suddenly, he said, "Stop. Don't move." He slipped his hand down and felt their joining. She moaned as he caressed her mound, then stiffened, and, with a gasp fell, onto him. He gripped her to him, driving into her with a growl, calling her name. Locked in a fierce embrace, drops of sweat covering her body, tears formed in Juana's eyes.

"I love you. I love you, my husband. How is it that I can be so lucky?"

"No, I am the lucky one. You are everything to me. I do not have the words to tell you how strong my love is. I do not ever want to be without you. You are mine. This is my gift to you, my wife." They sat completely still linked together, speechless, memorizing each other's face. The bells from the church rang but they did not hear them. The phone rang and rang and neither could think of answering it.

It was three months later and Juana had hurried down the hill from their house to open the restaurant for breakfast. A stitch in her side grew into an odd, twisting cramp. Her vision blurred and she fell onto a chair. Feeling faint, she laid her head on the cool tabletop. Recovering, she said aloud,

"I can't get sick right now. I'll stop at the doctor's tomorrow."

Hearing the happy news that she was to have a child, Juana counted back the months, and smiled to herself about the true gift given to her at Christmas.

Chapter 35

DONKEY RIDE – FIVE YEARS LATER

The fat donkey carrying two boys picked up speed on the cobblestone road doing down the hillside.

"Aaiiyee"! Go burro, go." The older boy in front was having a great time. The four year old holding on around his waist had his eyes closed tight. As they reached the corner at a speed the aged donkey only vaguely remembered, an old truck at the intersection honked loudly. The donkey jerked his head, skidded and stumbled on the stones. The boy holding on behind loosened his grip and he slid to the side. He felt his shoulder hit the ground, but did not feel the donkey's hoof clip his head with a glancing blow. The truck's rusty brakes screeched, the horn blew and the donkey brayed. The noise carried into the restaurant courtyard, causing a stir amongst those having lunch.

"Go see what has happened, Juana," said Hugo.

Juana looked out through the archway and said, "Only a boy and a donkey." Then she saw the boy kneeling over a small figure on the ground wearing a red shirt such as she had put on Fernando that morning. Alarmed, she ran across the road, "My son, my son. He is hurt!" She gathered him in her arms and carried him to the kitchen, laying him on the wood box. She felt his arms and legs and found a bump on his head.

"Get me a wet cloth." She laid the cloth on the side of his head carefully. "Wake up 'Nando. Open your eyes; it's Mama."

Hugo washed his own hands, and then those of his son. "Nothing seems broken and, he will be all right. All boys fall." But the boy did not wake.

"Hugo, we have to take him to the doctor. Send someone to get Carmen to come - now. She can close for us." Fernando was limp and seemed to be sleeping. He slept through the doctor's exam and the hospital x-ray. The doctor requested that he stay through the night, and Hugo and Juana stayed as well. Juana slept very little on a small cot by his bed, and Hugo snored in a sagging wooden chair. The doctor let them take him home the next morning, advising both parents to watch him well for any small sign of concussion. Juana bathed her lifeless boy, put on his nightclothes, and sat by his bed watching him until well after midnight.

"Juana, come to bed; he will wake in the morning." However, he did not wake that next day, or the day after that. Juana had taken him to Carmen's while she went to work, but on Sunday, Hugo said,

"Juana, I need you to work today, and I need Carmen too."

Wringing her hands, Juana objected, "I can't leave him, Hugo; I can't leave him."

"Then we will take him with us. Wrap him up in his blanket and bring his pillow. I know just what to do." After he opened the restaurant, Hugo took the top off the wood box, slid it between the box and the wall, and then removed the wood and stacked it to one side. He gathered up his limp and silent son, with all the blankets and settled him in the box in the kitchen.

"There, my wife, you can see him and look at him all during the day. No harm will come to him. He will be just fine."

Brunch was over, and the dozen or so brilliantly costumed Huichol Indians were settled in the courtyard on their own blankets, finishing their packets of lunch. Though they did not buy much except for cold drinks and tortillas, they were always welcome. They brought laughter, music and a colorful spread of handmade wares to offer to customers and tourists. Wherever there were Huichols, there is music, though sometimes their energy and efforts were not quite as melodic as one would wish.

After eating, two Indian men took up their instruments; violin and a reed flute. A younger boy played two drums between his knees and two women shook rattles and scraped a hollow gourd. The younger children danced in a circle, and one young boy carried a small violin. The beat was infectious; the customers were smiling, clapping and tapping their feet. The sweet, high notes of the violin soared through the air. Fernando's eyes fluttered and opened. He had heard the violin and murmured,

"Play Papa. Play."

But this time it was not his Papa. Hugo was looking out the barn door with his back to Fernando. When he turned, he saw his son standing, looking over the edge of the wood box.

"Fernando, my boy! You are awake." He picked him up blankets and all and strode out to the patio.

"Juana, Carmen! Look, he is awake. I told you he would be fine."

Juana, her eyes reddened by lack of sleep and worry, touched and patted her son.

"Thank you Mother Mary, my prayers were heard. He is smiling. My son is awake. Are you hungry Fernando?"

Fernando rubbed his eyes and stretched his hands out to the boy with the small violin. "Violina, Mama, Violina, Papa."

The young Indian boy stopped dancing and held the violin behind his back, stepping behind his father. Fernando kept reaching for it. Hugo motioned to the father and the two men stepped to one side. The Indian explained that his own grandfather had made this violin. His grandfather and the uncle made violins in their village and all the children learned to play. It belonged to the young boy who would not learn to play; he just liked to carry it and did not want to part with it. He went on to say that the violin was old and had two broken strings. Hugo increased his offer. Within a few minutes, Fernando had his first violin. The Huichol wrapped the violin in a woven sack and the small bow separately in a ragged towel. It was a happy child who went to sleep with the violin by his side.

Hugo was secretly pleased. "Juana, I will take Fernando to Guadalajara next week and get new strings. I will look for a small case. I think it is good that he wants to play the violin like his Papa."

Chapter 36

GUATEMALA

Ramos couldn't remember when he was the youngest of the family. In the beginning of the happy marriage of his mother and father, they began having children right away. They came regularly two or three years apart – two boys, then two girls, then Ramos, then another boy, then another girl, but she was not to be the last child as his mother was heavily pregnant again.

The hard packed dirt yard was always filled with children, some who lived in the plain two bedroom house and many who didn't. Ramos was almost nine and not quite old enough to work in the fields all day with his father and two older brothers, but he soon would be.

Ramos had the large easy smile of his father and his mother's patience. His good nature made him popular in the neighborhood as he was always available to help build fences, move heavy rocks and even find lost children with no complaints.

The family lived at the edge of the village of San Marcos, Guatemala, in the poor section of town with a lean-to made of branches for the sleeping quarters of the two oldest boys. There was only one road through their neighborhood that ended in the woods. A trail behind the house led into the dense trees and eventually came upon a sparkling stream that Ramos couldn't quite jump across. With only twittering birds and bushy tailed squirrels to see him fail, he tried and tried and came up short and of course very wet. He knew he would make it soon. He promised himself many things would happen when he could jump across the stream. He would quit school and go to work with his father. He would start out early one morning and walk the miles to the end of the lake where he had heard it was so shallow even families could cross and cross illegally into Mexico.. But first he would follow the smiling brown haired girl to her house just to see where she lived, of course. Then the money he made working for his father would start the savings for his trip to the Estados Unidos. His oldest brother almost had enough money and had bought a canoe and hidden it in the forest to sneak across the big river into the state of Chiapas, Mexico, on his journey through Mexico to the United States. This was the dream of most of the boys in the village and some did go and were never heard of again, but several had been sending money orders to the town post office over the years and when mail came in, the shout came through the streets, "letter here, letter here."

The day came when his mother grabbed his shoulder hard and said they had to go to the clinic so she could have her baby. They walked to the road, waited for the bus and got off at the clinic without a word spoken. She went with the nurse but looked back and said quietly, "Stay here, don't worry."

A few hours later, the doctor looked at the pale child born silent. "I am so sorry Senora; this little girl just could not breathe. And you, you should stay here tonight. How many other children do you have?"

She held up six fingers.

The doctor sighed, "Do you want more children? You should not have any more; you are not strong enough to hold them."

She turned her head into the pillow with tears in her eyes, after a few moments, whispered "No."

The doctor filled out a paper and had her sign, saying, "Have your husband sign this as well and I will be able to do this small thing."

The tired mother looked at the doctor and said, "My husband cannot write. Take it to my son and he will put down the name."

Ramos did jump the stream, followed the girl to her home, trekked down the river, known as the Usamacinto, went to work with his father and saved his money for years. His oldest brother used the canoe to slip into Mexico and found work in the coffee fields of

Chiapas. He came back every Christmas for a visit. His second oldest brother walked to the end of the river and crossed into Mexico going west to the coast. He sent two letters and then no more.

It was time. The dream that had filled his mind since childhood was raging to begin. Ramos kissed his mother goodbye and told her he was going across the river to work in the coffee fields. Of course, that was not his true destination, but just the beginning.

Chapter 37

THE BOLILLO MAKER – 1971

Rosa got up every day at four in the morning, when it was deep black out of her windows, to start the dough for the bolillos. The nearby restaurant and two small stores depended on her for the freshly baked yeast rolls. She had three large sacks ready to go by 6:30 a.m. and called to her son.

"Miguel, get up, you will be late getting to school. You have to deliver the rolls and the restaurant opens at seven." Miguel was coughing when she went into the bedroom.

"Mama, I am sick." She felt his forehead - it was hot to her touch and he was perspiring.

"Open your mouth… let me see your throat. It looks very red. I think you should stay home. I will get you some tea with honey."

She left her sixteen year old deep under the blankets and set off to deliver her fresh rolls.

First, she set a bag on the counter outside the doors and knocked, in case anyone was there. She walked quickly down the road where roof dogs greeted her approach. It was light when she reached her third customer, a very small corner store. She handed the rolls to the ancient woman behind the counter and received her pesos, giving some back as she bought a few items. Noticing a stocky young man sweeping the store and on out into the street, she greeted him in passing.

"Buena Dias."

Flashing an enormous smile, he answered, "Buena Dias, senorita. Would it be possible you might have some work for me? I can do everything, yard work, tree cutting, and house painting. I work for very little, just a small meal and a few pesos for cigarettes."

Rosa blushed, replying, "I am not a senorita. I have a son." She hesitated, "I do have some trees and bushes in my yard that need cutting, and brush that needs burning."

The handsome young man stood the broom in a corner, said goodbye and hugged the storeowner. She thanked him and handed him a cigarette and a banana.

He followed Rosa out of the store, and on the half mile walk to her home she learned of his many brothers and sisters in San Marcos, Guatemala and his harrowing trip north. It was his intent to travel further north to find work in the United States.

"A priest helped me in Tapachula – giving me an address to go to in Tijuana, of the Casa Del Migrante."

"What is your name?"

He answered with a grin, "Just call me Ramos."

The first week he cut trees and burned brush. The second week he dug a garden. The third week, he and Miguel built a barbecue out of broken bricks and rocks. The fourth week, he and Miguel swept, watered and cleaned the slate walkways of the motel. They became a threesome, going everywhere together, settling in almost like a family. Four weeks of proximity, yard work, visits to the plaza, laughter and talking, taking all their meals together, forged their friendship. The fifth week, he slept with Rosa. The sixth week on a Sunday Ramos asked Rosa to take a walk with him to the lake.

"Rosa, you are a good woman and I like your son, but you know my dream is still to go north. I want to work and travel in the United States. I want to see other places. That has been my dream, since I was a boy. I have to do this."

She looked out over the green-brown water and the waves curling steadfastly and at last answered, saying, "I thought you might stay. When are you going?"

He took her hand, "Tomorrow."

Rosa fixed a special dinner and packed a big bag of food. Sometime in the night she felt Ramos leave the bed quietly. Rosa, her throat choked, said nothing, moving over to the warm spot he had left, pressed her face into his pillow and whispered to herself, "Come back, Ramos, please come back."

A month later, Rosa found that she was pregnant.

Chapter 38

MARINA FALLS

Carmen's teenage daughter, Marina hated the bus ride home after school. She did not have the excitement for Friday as the others. She was going to her after-school job to help Juana set up chairs at the restaurant for a club meeting. She boarded heavily, sitting in front on the long wide seat. Boys and girls pushed and shoved their way to the much preferred back seats, out of sight of the bus driver. Laughing and taunting one another, they made fun of the couples who sat together.

One of the girls whispered behind her hand, "Oh Roberto, hug me, kiss me, just once. I won't tell." Boys standing in the aisle leaned precariously over the girls, waiting for the bus to lurch so they could pretend to fall in their laps.

"Oops, sorry - as long as I am here, how about it?" Erica, who was popular with the boys because of her large breasts, and who allowed them to look up her skirts, laughed and giggled when Jose fell headfirst in her lap. He kissed the back of his own hand, making loud smacking noises,

"Erica, let me be your baby; feed me Mommy, yum, yum."

The bus driver growled, "All right you guys, keep it down back there. Stay in your own seat or get off the bus."

Marina pulled herself up by the post and swung carefully down the first step, waiting to get off at the Gallo Loco corner. Marina was large, very large. Delicate features were buried between round cheeks and a triple chin. Fat hung on her arms over her wrists like a long blouse. Her bulk and weight made her a continual target of jokes. Two of the boys scuffled and pressed behind her, and, as the door opened they fell against each other pushing Marina out the door and down on one knee in the gravel roadside. The two ran off laughing as Miguel jumped out and helped her up.

"Are you hurt? Your knee is bleeding, come over and sit down." He led her under the tree in the courtyard to the picnic bench saying, "Put your foot up on this chair, and hold this handkerchief here, not hard, just to keep the blood from dripping. I will get some water."

Dolores, who was watching from the doorway of her motel, called out, "Can I help? Anything I can do?"

"Can I wash my hands in your place?" After scrubbing his hands clean with soap, Miguel filled a glass with soapy water and grabbed some paper napkins. He sat by Marina and said,

"I am going to pour water over your knee to clean off the dirt and gravel. If it hurts, bite on your thumb. Don't worry, I am going to be a doctor someday, and you are my first patient." The water cleaned most of the scrape. He was supporting her knee with one hand and picked out the gravel pieces, as he said, "You will be fine. You have good skin and will heal fast."

Marina said nothing throughout the cleaning. It did hurt, but all she could think of was how near Miguel was. It was embarrassing to have him bend over her leg, his breath fluttering her plaid school skirt. His hands were rough and warm where he touched the sensitive skin behind her knee. Occasionally, his bare arm would touch the skin of her leg. A warm flush rose from her neck to her hair. Just then, the rooster crowed from his perch up in the tree above. Miguel, seeing her clenched hands, and hoping to take Marina's mind off the pain, began to talk about the rooster.

"He is a crazy rooster. Roosters just don't crow in the morning you know. He crows when there is danger to his lady chickens. He thinks they are all his. He would chase another rooster away, even a dog too. Maybe he is worried about us. Someone named him Rooster because he roosts at night."

The flush had passed, but Marina's voice was still mute. She was only half listening. New and amazing feelings were overwhelming her. She wanted to touch his shiny black curls as he leaned close to her knee. She didn't want this closeness, this warmth and attention, to end. Juana had come out and hurriedly gone back in to get her first aid box for spray and band aids.

"Don't worry about the chairs, Marina. Here, spray this Bactine on it."

Miguel placed a gauze piece over the knee, securing it at each end with tape. "That is to keep it clean. Just take it easy walking for a while." He finished and stood up, dusting off his knees. Her eyelids flickered and closed and the sudden lack of his touch caused an unbidden single tear to trickle down her cheek. Thanking Miguel, she got up carefully. Miguel took her arm, helping her up.

Leaning over, he kissed her check, "You were my first patient. I am your doctor now and I say go home and rest your knee."

Marina walked slowly up the hill, her thoughts confused. She went over every moment that had happened. First the fall, then the water over the knee, then Miguel picking out the gravel, breathing on her skin, his rough hands lightly scraping her leg, and then the kiss. She went over it again, limping up the hill and into her house. She went into her bedroom and shut the door to be alone so she could think about it again. Her mother had seen her limp in and asked what happened.

"It's not too bad Mama, I just fell down and scraped my knee. I'm going to lie down."

"It's time to eat; can I bring you a plate?"

"No Mama, I am not hungry."

After dinner her mother came to the door and said, "Do you want to feed Pepita?"

Each night the remains of dinner went out to the black faced milk goat in the back yard. Marina always took out the plate, delicately tasting this bit or this piece of leftover. Sometimes the scraps that finally got to the goat were half of what she had when she started out.

This night Marina answered, "No, let Ruby do it, she's big enough now." With raised eyebrows, Carmen gave the plate to an exuberant sister.

Marina went to bed early that night thinking of each word that had been said, the touch of his hands, and the kiss, the first kiss from anyone other than her family. Her thoughts were spinning, and she knew she was different now. Everything she did from then on would be different. Everything. Marina lost a pound that night but no one knew. In the morning she looked carefully at her face in the mirror to see if anything showed she had changed. True to her promise to do everything different, she had fruit for breakfast and black coffee - no big breakfast and no rich goat milk. That day she lost two pounds. For the rest of the next week she got up earlier, half ran down the hill toward the highway, and walked to school instead of taking the bus, eager and hopeful that she would run into Miguel when he was delivering bolillos. That week she lost eight more pounds. She looked for him on the way to their secondary school, and looked for him at school though he was not in any of her classes as he was two years ahead. The days she went to the restaurant after school, she was nervous doing her work, fixated on only one thing; seeing him again. It was almost an obsession. How would it be? Would he smile and talk to her as if nothing had happened, or would he ignore her? After all, she was the one everyone made fun of. Each night she ate lightly, going to her room early to think everything over again, and especially the kiss, that marvelous kiss. Would it ever happen again? Even a week later, repeating the story in her head, the part about the kiss still made her shiver.

Chapter 39

TIME FOR HOMEWORK

The school bus was crowded with students acting up and laughing. One girl was held on by two boys long after her stop. First she giggled and then complained. Marina was glad that it was her turn to get off, but sorry that she had not seen Miguel. Three months had passed since her skinned knee. She had run down the hill early and walked fast quickly to school each day, hoping to run into him. From the moment she woke, the main thought filling her head was to see Miguel, just to be near him. They had walked together several times, sometimes talking, sometimes not. Once he had let her carry the bag of fresh bolillos that his mother had baked, to the little store. Twice when she was working in the restaurant, he had come and sat at an outside table to do his homework, saying that he had no time when he got home as he had to take care of his little brother. She had helped him with his homework. She had lost 46 pounds and her chin was firm and her throat was flat. Her mother had taken her skirts in several times, not saying anything, and with her mouth full of pins, just basted her skirts smaller.

Marina asked Juana what she could do for her that day. "Not much today, just clear and straighten the outside tables, pick some limes and check the garden to see if there are any ripe tomatoes." Marina picked a basket of limes, and as she straightened the tables, saw Miguel's blue shirt enter the chayote field and fade quickly out of sight.

A puzzled look crossed her face. On the seat of one of the white plastic chairs she spied his school notebook with his name, "Dr. Miguel Chavez" spiraled and double lined in black across the front.

She called in to Juana, "I'm done. I'm going." Grabbing the notebook, she headed for the trellised field. Leaves and bruised squash covered the ground; trailing vines flew in her face as she followed the disturbed debris. Stopping to listen, she heard him kicking through the leaves and hurried behind him. She burst into the clearing and saw him sitting on an old sleeping bag.

"What are you doing, following me?"

Breathing heavily, she answered, "You left your homework book. I just brought it. What are you doing in here?"

"Sometimes I take a little sleep before I go home and babysit my brother. My Mama leaves when I get home and works late; he keeps me busy. I have to feed him, clean him up and put him to bed. That is why I do my homework first. Thanks for the book. Do you want to sit down?" They talked about his little brother, - he called him Junior. He told her about the time he had broken his arm when he was ten. That was when he decided to be a doctor and that's why he decided to go to college. Marina talked about her sixteenth birthday coming soon, and the party her parents were having for her at their house. He kept stealing sideways glances at her, hoping she would not see him. Unconsciously, they had moved closer together. When the sun passed over the edge of the vines behind them, he said,

"I'm late, I've got to go!"

Getting up, he pulled her close to him in a tight grip. He looked into her face, then down to her breasts saying, "You're looking pretty good lately, Marina," and kissed her fully on the mouth. His lips were full and soft and the kiss was gentle. Her heart was pounding; she could hear his breathing. Her arms went around him and she pressed closer. A tingling started in her stomach, and when his tongue parted her lips and touched hers, the blood pounded in her head and her body trembled. Her eager response surprised him, so he pushed himself into her soft curves. His tongue explored her mouth, and Marina welcomed the heat that filled her senses and made her knees weak.

He broke their embrace, holding her away from him saying, "I really have to go, but meet me here tomorrow." With a quick kiss on her forehead, he turned and ran through the vines.

Marina stumbled out of the backside of the field, almost walking into an old man riding on the rump of a heavily laden donkey. Small blue darting birds flew over her head but she didn't see them. Her steps stirred up small whirlwinds of warm dust as she slowly, instinctively headed for home. This new sensation filled her completely. She shook her head to focus her eyes and smiled inwardly as she accepted her future. One hour ago, she was a child and because of a brief moment of surprising affection, she was surely a woman.

Chapter 40

ARE YOU A GHOST?

It was closing time and Rosa packed up the few bolillos she had left. The cheese and yogurt shop owner let her have a small counter at the back of his shop finding that her bread and rolls complimented his products. She had avoided his offers to take her to dinner, so far. She just wanted to be friends. She left bread for him in exchange for a few cheese slices.

She and the shoe shop woman always had a small dinner before she walked home. Counting her coins, she could see it was almost enough for a new pair of huaraches for Miguel. After their meal, Rosa handed her left over rolls to the old woman sitting on the ground beside the restaurant.

It was dark when she opened her door to see Miguel sleeping on the sofa with a book in his hand. 'I'm home – is Junior asleep? Go to bed now." Rosa locked up the house and took a shower. Getting ready for bed she heard a noise on the porch. She thought she heard a light knock. Then the knocking came again, harder this time.

"Who is it? Hurriedly putting on a robe, she peeped out the tiny window in the door and saw a man's figure. "Who is it?"

The figure spoke, "It's me - it's Ramos."

She slammed the peep hole window shut, "Madre Dios! Are you sure? Are you a ghost?

"It's me, Rosa, tired and hungry."

She threw the door open and put her arms around him.

"Ramos, my Ramos. You came back. You are here. I am so happy."

"I have come a long way today. Let me sit down. Could I have some water, or something to drink?" Rosa hurried to the kitchen bringing a cola, bolillos, ham and cheese.

Ramos took off his dusty jacket, his worn shoes and accepted the food with a grateful smile. Between bites, he talked,

"I wanted to come back to you Rosa. First, I went to San Diego and worked at a cemetery. Then three of us hitched rides to Arizona and got jobs at a golf course. After that, we did everything. We picked strawberries, fruit, whatever there was. We made a little money. Two of us came back together on the bus and stopped a few times to pick melons and corn. We rode busses but walked a lot too." His voice trailed off and his eyelids drooped. He fell asleep sitting up. Rosa covered him with a blanket and gazed at him for a long time. A cold spot in her heart had melted. Kissing him softly, she thought of their son now almost two years old, she whispered into his hair,

"You will have a big surprise, tomorrow."

Chapter 41

THE PACT

The day of the kiss in the chayote field was the beginning for Marina and Miguel. They began to walk to school together, and study their homework under the jacaranda tree. Months went by and their companionship became more than friendship and was noticed. The feeling between them was mutual and they always had things to say to each other.. They spoke and talked as if they were had been good friends for years. He was excited to tell her that he was accepted for college the next fall and that Dolores was taking him to a motel keeper's conference in Guadalajara the next Sunday to meet other hotel owners who might help him. He could give yard care and maintenance in exchange for a place to stay during the week. She asked him how he felt about her taking the preparatory courses to become a nurse.

Their kisses became hotter and deeper though they always stopped short of "going all the way".

Marina continued to lose weight and by that time, everyone noticed. They were going into the chayote field several times a week.

Miguel was laying on top of Marina on the weathered sleeping bag, crunching leaves and chayote fruit as he moved his long legs on her again and again, pushing the noticeable mark of his manhood roughly into the vee between her thighs through her clothes. Marina moved quickly onto her side.

"Oh stop, Miguel; we must stop."

Marina had earnestly promised her mother that she would be a virgin until she married, though the promise was made years ago by a fat girl oblivious to the fact that a boy would ever be interested in her.

She pleaded, "We just can't! You know we can't."

Groaning and rolling over onto his back, Miguel replied, "I know. I know. We will just do other things. We will wait. We can just kiss and hold each other."

So their pact was agreed upon. They would kiss, touch, and look, and that was all. Miguel laid his head in her lap and said in a muffled tone,

"Are you my girlfriend?'

"Yes, yes. I want to be. I guess I am. You don't know, but I have been in my heart since the day you fixed my knee."

Miguel turned in her lap looking into her eyes over the curve of her breasts and said in a whisper, "Marina, let me touch you."

Marina looked at him solemnly, and closed her eyes, slowly pulling her blouse out of her skirt. His fingers lightly caressed her creamy skin, fitting both hands around one soft breast as she bent to him. His eager mouth closed over the dark, silky circle. His tongue first touched her nipple, sucking gently, then harder. A lightning bolt of powerful pleasure started at his touch, flying and zigzagging down to her most private part. Marina stiffened her back, pulling away from his mouth.

"Oh, please let me; you are so beautiful." His breath was warm on her skin. He whispered brokenly, "You know what this does to me."

Her answer was, "We should stop."

Miguel sat up, arranged her clothing and saying earnestly, "Will you wait for me to finish medical school? It will be a few years. Will you wait until I become a doctor and we can get married?"

Marina's eyes filled with tears, relief and gladness flooding through her. She nodded her head, "Yes, of course I will wait for you."

The next morning at breakfast, Marina told her family that she would like to go to prep school and then college to become a nurse.

Chapter 42

FIRST SUNDAY IN JANUARY – 1983

Linda, Maigret and Juana sat in silence at the picnic table. The table seemed incomplete without Bernie. Linda sighed, "I guess I am just not as hungry as I used to be. I should have paid more attention when Bernie said she wasn't feeling well. She always felt good. What does that mean anyway, when you say you are 'off middle'? I miss her."

Maigret replied, "No one could have known. We all miss her. She was my best friend."

Two months had gone by since Bernie passed away peacefully in her sleep. Linda missed her every day as she did things they had done together, eating breakfast on the patio, shopping, planning a garden, and even taking naps at the same time. The bond of friendship the two women shared had grown strong since she had moved in, and unconsciously they had become more and more dependent on each other. Manny and Carmen had helped her through the funeral, putting Bernie's ashes in the small Mexican cemetery next to Harlan's. Linda was grateful they that they had had a wonderful dinner at home on her last night and a long conversation after dinner sitting on the patio observing and appreciating the many moods of the lake below. Specifically Bernie discussed at length the recent remarkable and moving recital, and mentioned how glad she was to see, and for others to see, Linda's obvious relationship with Fernando. Bernie was enthusiastic about her idea to turn the White House into a B & B and about how Linda and Fernando would be a big help in that business.

Carmen and Marina had come for several days to help sort things and clean house. Linda moved her things from the upstairs bedroom next to where Bernice had slept to the smaller, main level bedroom where she felt more at ease.

Linda busied herself with small daily things: housework, visits from friends, working in the yard, playing her violin, making freezer jam out of the local fruit, and just spending restful times on the patio appreciating the lake. She enjoyed her memories of Bernice but her thoughts seemed always to come back to Fernando. In her last will, Bernie had specifically mentioned Linda was to have all of her personal effects, including her jewelry, and she remembered the small blue velvet jewel case in the dresser. Linda was delighted to find a wide, gold wedding band with the inscription 'True Love' engraved inside. She wondered aloud if this ring was meant for her, then a faint echo spun through her head, and she thought she heard Bernice saying, "Yes, this is your ring now, Linda."

Fernando had quietly spent two weekends with her, telling his mother he had to stay at school for study and tests. During those weekends they visited other B & B's to see and talk with the owners and managers to encourage and strengthen their resolve, born of Bernie's wish in her last will to make the White House into a beautiful Bed and Breakfast.

Chapter 43

JUST A SMALL WEDDING IN JUNE – 1983

In the months after Bernie's death, Juana could see Fernando and Linda growing closer. He was spending more time at the White House, sometimes doing his homework and always taking his violin. Her attitude toward the young people showed a face of unhappiness and disapproval bubbled just below the surface. It was expected, but still a shock when Fernando told her that he had taken Linda to the priest to talk about a wedding in June.

"It will be just a small wedding, Mama… in the priest's office. I need you to be there with me, and maybe Carmen. The next day we will go to the Notary Public to change the ownership of the house and apply for all the permits needed to open it as a small hotel. Are you happy for me Mama? I will be married to a beautiful girl, have my own home and a college education to run our business. I have to thank you for pushing me to stay in school, and for everything else you have done for me. I would be nothing without you," he said, taking her in his arms and squeezing her.

Time sailed by and the wedding day came. It was to be Sunday evening after the restaurant had closed.

In the small church, with its flickering votive prayer candles and softly brilliant stained glass windows, the bride to be clutched Fernando's arm, shivering occasionally, though not from cold, as they waited for the priest. She wore a simple pale green dress and lace head scarf and he wore the traditional black pants and snowy white pleated wedding shirt. The priest waved them into his office, leaving Juana waiting outside in the polished pew. A few minutes later he called her in and asked her to stand with the couple. Suddenly, there was a knocking, and Juana looked up,

"That could be Carmen." But it was the church caretaker with a surprised look on his face saying, "Father, people are coming." As they looked out, they could see that it was Carmen, but also her husband Manny, and Ruby, and behind them came Marina and Miguel, now married. Ruby, as tall as her mother, Carmen, stood at the side of the church playing softly on her violin. The neighbors who lived between Carmen and Juana were there too, as well as dozens of their regular patrons at the restaurant with their families, Dolores and her new friend, Paulo, with big smiles on their faces, came and sat near the front. Rosa , Ramos and their son, Junior, were there and even the farmer who owned the chayote field. Dolores stepped up and pinned a dewy corsage of green and brown cymbidium orchids on Linda's shoulder.

With a laugh of surprise, the priest said, "It looks like we are having our wedding out in the church."

He and Fernando went out, but Juana laid her hand on Linda's arm. "Stay with me for a moment. I need to talk with you." Facing her, looking steadily into Linda's eyes, she said quietly,

"Do you love my son?"

With a sweet smile, the answer came confidently, "With all my heart."

"You need to like him, as well as love him. What do you like about my son?"

Linda closed her eyes and spoke, "I like it when he walks next to me on the street, walking tall with his head up. I like his laugh and how sometimes, he even giggles. I like his face and his big smile when he greets friends and the way he kisses me on each cheek when we meet. I like when he gives a coin to a beggar or picks up a crying child. I like that he is a wonderful musician and the way he teaches violin, making it easy. I think he is kind and has a generous heart. Most of all, I like the way he speaks of you, telling me how proud he is of you and all you have done."

Juana sighed, "Yes, he has always been a kind and generous boy."

With a wry smile, Linda answered, "He is a kind and generous man, Juana, not a boy."

Studying Juana's face, she went on, "But I love him for the man he will be in the future, by my side, the business man, the hotel owner, my husband, and perhaps a father. I respect and admire him. There has been a hole in my heart since my mother died, and he fills that hole, encouraging me to be more than I am. I want to be more because of him. He is my first love and my best friend. I can't imagine my life without him. He is what he is because of you. I feel I have a purpose here, a connection with a family."

A smiling Juana took off the white scarf Linda was wearing, reached into her bag, and pulled out a filmy, floral scarf that her mother had left her, "I'd like you to wear this. I wore it at my own wedding. I want you to know a saying we have in our country. It is, 'When the dust of Mexico, falls upon your heart, you will never be the same.' Here, take my arm and let's walk out together."

Maigret had brought a beautiful wedding cake, and Miguel had brought a dozen long stemmed, perfect yellow roses. After the wedding, the guests gathered in the church entry room talking and laughing. Hugs and kisses and handshakes and happy congratulations were showered on the bride and groom. Maigret gathered up the scraps of cake and secured it in a small box for Linda to take home. Fernando made sure that everyone knew they were going away on a two day honeymoon, but just where a secret – not even Linda knew..

Just before they left, Fernando took Maigret aside for a hurried, whispered conversation, then sped with Linda through the empty Sunday streets to their home, La Casa Blanca, the White House.

Fernando lifted her across the threshold and carried her into their bedroom. He took off her clothes, piece by piece, very slowly, and only when her shoes were off did she feel naked and begin to tremble. His hands moved over her body gently, "Lie down with me, my wife, and let me show you how I love you. For the first time, together, in complete happiness, to share the bed we will share for the rest of our lives. If I ever lived before, I loved you then. If I ever live again, it will be you that I love."

Linda woke before dawn, and opened her eyes, stretching and yawning. First she looked at her golden wedding band and then at the handsome man sleeping next to her, his face at rest, his eyelashes long and dark, his hair tousled and curly. Pleased and happy with the sweet and sensual memories of the last night darting through her head, she watched him sleep. She thought of how much she loved him and how everything was going to turn out well with them together. She was filled with happiness and thankful for the events that had brought her to the day. Fernando had whispered in her ear just before they went to sleep that their honeymoon was to be right here in their own home, perfectly private, just the two of them. Tugging on a thick robe, she filled the coffee pot, and while it was percolating, opened the double doors to the patio to wait for the inevitable magnificent sunrise.

Chapter 44

RAINY SEASON – 1983

The Sunday Brunch was the same delicious feast as always, and the women still spoke of their Amiga, Bernice, who had passed away quietly in her sleep the year before. In her will she had chosen Linda Lou Campbell, to inherit and care for the big white house known as Casa Blanca. Linda Lou and Fernando had worked tirelessly to clean, paint and update the huge home of glistening white stucco boasting Moorish domed towers, huge rooms and three tiled patios, each with an awesome view of Lake Chapala. A month before their work was almost completed; Linda Lou and Fernando Alvarez had been married in the nearby church.

Linda Lou and Maigret brought their plates to the long table under the jacaranda tree. Since Maigret had been living with Russell on the lake front, they didn't see each other as often.

Maigret shivered and buttoned her sweater,

"This may be our last brunch outdoors, Linda. The rains are going to start soon. Actually, my baking business improves when it's cooler. I don't know why. I brought Tiramisu today, I know you like it. After lunch I am going to Chapala and check for mail."

Linda spoke, "I am so going to enjoy this lunch. We are ready for the rain. Doesn't it seem to rain mostly at night? All we have left to do at the house is cleaning outside, planting bushes and things. The greenhouse people are bringing them tomorrow. Then we can start painting the inside while Fernando is at school. This is his last year. You know, Bernice was really the one who had the idea of making the house into a Bed and Breakfast. Our apartment behind the kitchen is finished and as soon as we finish painting, we could open. Should we have some kind of a grand opening party? Pass me the guacamole."

Loud motors passed by in a roar on the road then came back again. Three people came in through the multi-colored archway…two men and a boy. They sat down, and the burly person with the handlebar mustache shouted to the server,

"Beer me, and hurry up about it. Make it three."

The smaller person, who at second glance, turned out to be a petite mud-splattered female, answered back, "No beer for me, just a coke. I'm going in to wash up."

The two men, dressed in leather pants and jackets, had their heads together, laughing and talking when the server brought three beers and a coke. Mustache man laughed,

"No problem, I can drink two. In fact, bring another for my buddy." Slapping his friend on the back, he bent closer and whispered loudly, "Stan, my man, women are no damn good. Once you get a woman involved with a ride, everything goes gunnysack. They want to do everything their own way. That old gal of mine was bugging me for two hundred miles. She should have known it's my way… or the highway."

"Yeah, but that was pretty cold, dropping her off at the airport."

"I gave her money for a ticket, didn't I? She can go back to California or not. I didn't want to argue with her anymore and I think you should do the same. What do you see in that skinny Lola anyway? We could have some fine times if it was just you and me. Don't forget who is financing this ride. Come on, this is as good a place as any. Grab your beer and let's vamoose before she comes back." He stood up and threw some bills on the table and the two hurried out.

The rumble of two motorcycles rocketed over the hedge just as the young girl came through the door. Her red hair, short and spiky, dripped water on her denim jacket. Standing by her coke on the table, she looked around for the two men. Frowning, she sat and drank her coke almost in one gulp. She went to the flower covered archway entrance and looked out.

Maigret looked at Linda Lou and shook her head, "This doesn't look good."

Linda was blissfully chewing Chile Relleno with her eyes half closed, "I need this recipe; the egg batter around the cheesy pepper is just heaven. What did you say? You are right; this looks like trouble, for her anyway. Here she comes."

Head down, the small, wiry person walked hesitantly toward them, "Ah, did you see those two guys leave?"

Linda Lou looked up at clear hazel eyes in a shiny face dotted with freckles. "Yes, and we heard them too. Were you with them?"

The red head declared, "*I am* with them. I just wondered if they said anything about going somewhere – to the store maybe."

Maigret shook her head, "No, all I heard was about dropping someone at the airport. Sit down, you might as well sit and talk while you wait. Have some chips and salsa."

"Thanks. My name is Lola. We're on a ride from California. We've been to Oaxaca and are heading back north. There was another girl, but she and her boyfriend had an argument so we took her to the airport this morning. We wanted to see the lake so we came this way. They should be coming back." Her eyes lit up when she heard motorcycles in the distance.

"See, I knew Stan would be back." The sound of the motors stopped and a backpack and bedroll flew through the arch, bouncing across flagstones to land against a potted plant near the door. Guttural laughter sounded as a beer bottle careened over the hedge and spiraled crazily on the flagstones. The shout came over the growl of departing motors, "Sayonara baby!"

Lola jumped up and ran to the street, calling after the cyclists in the distance. "Wait! Come back. Come back! You can't leave me here!" Minutes later, grim and unsmiling, she slumped down beside her backpack, head in her hands, and elbows on the knees of her torn jeans.

"Now what am I going to do?" A teardrop rolled down beside her nose. Then another and just then a raindrop mixed in with the tears. Lola, looking up, saw the older couple at the next table struggling to put on their sweaters. Jumping up, she went to their table, saying,

"I'll take your plates inside, you go on in." She efficiently cleaned their table, and set them up inside. After grabbing a dishpan off a hook by the door, she quickly piled all the dirty dishes from the two tables as Linda Lou and Maigret were bringing their plates and everything they could carry inside. Everyone was safe inside as the cloudburst continued. Thanking Lola, Juana said,

"You have a job with me anytime, Amiga. You have done this before."

Lola grinned wryly, "Thanks, I may need it. I worked my way through high school bussing tables, that and working in a garden shop." Digging in her backpack, she cried out, "He took my money, all my pesos. That rat bastard, now what will I do."

Linda Lou looked intently at the dejected Lola, remembering the first time she had entered the same courtyard in distress, then spoke. "Sit down a minute. Let's talk. You say you worked in a garden shop, with flowers, planting and things like that?"

"Taking care of flowers, planting from seed, mowing lawns, planting, mixing compost, digging, just about everything. I learned a lot about what flowers go where and which ones like each other."

Linda shook her head up and down vigorously, "Do you know what you are doing, I mean, are you really good."

"Oh yes, I worked for them for almost five years. They liked my work and would take me full time when I was ready. I was heading there when I stopped for coffee and met the guys on the motorcycles."

Linda raised her eyebrows as she looked closely at Maigret. Maigret smiled and shrugged her shoulders.

Linda spoke slowly, "This is really a coincidence. This may be sudden, but what do you think about this idea? I have a little house you could stay in for a while. My idea is that you work for me for board and room. I'm opening a bed and breakfast soon and I have a load of shrubs and flowers coming tomorrow and I really need help. My husband is at school five days a week in Guadalajara, and I sure don't know what to do with them. On Sunday he helps his mother at the restaurant until they close. The little house is not clean…it's packed with furniture while we are painting, but we could try it for a couple of weeks."

A huge smile spread across Lola's face. She stood up and Linda saw that the words on her faded t-shirt read, "Gone with the Wind". Sticking out her hand quickly, she said, "I'll shake on that!"

The casita was jammed with furniture every which way. There was a narrow walkway in between piled boxes. Linda started moving dining room chairs piled upside down on the couch.

"I'm not even going to try to get into the bedroom today, so you will have to sleep on the couch tonight. We can clear out some of these boxes."

"At least I'll be inside. That's a whole lot better than what I've been doing for the last two weeks. It will be just fine."

Linda burrowed through several cardboard boxes, "Let's start by setting up my kitchen. There should be three boxes marked "L's kitchen". Ah, here they are. Grab one and let's take them up to the house."

They unpacked boxes, washed all the cutlery and dishes, and filled drawers and cupboards working in cheerful companionship. Linda found her box of curtains and they covered the windows and then made up the couch with fresh linen for Lola. They hardly noticed the time passing as Laurel talked of her life and how she came to Mexico. Linda suggested a stop for tea and crackers. She brought the tea, crackers and slices of crumbly white cheese. By then they were sitting on the small patio in front of the casita. Even the patio of the casita had a good view of the lake.

"I lived in an orphanage till I was eighteen. They say I was left on the doorstep when I was about three months old. I don't really know my birthday, they just gave me one. There was a penciled note that said my name was Laurel, not Lola. That was just something that Stan, my biker friend, my ex friend, stuck on me. All the kids in our house were called Smith, so I am Laurel Smith. Pretty much everybody in our town knew where you came from if your name was Smith. The orphanage asked you to work when you could, so I did work and saved some money. I started bussing tables in the eighth grade. Then I went to the greenhouse one summer and just stayed there, working all during high school. Smith House was proud when anybody graduated and I did. A few months later I was eighteen, so they packed me up, gave me my money, and showed me the door. That was the day I went to the coffee shop on my way to the greenhouse, and then along comes Stan and his motorcycle. You know the rest."

"How long can you stay? Do you want to go back?"

With her chin up and with a determined look on her face, she said, "I don't have anything to go back to."

Linda asked Laurel, "You are young but you have grown up pretty fast. Do you know what you want to do with your life? I mean, school, job, where do you want to live?"

Laurel gulped and her chin quivered, looking away from Linda, "I want to do what I do best and that is gardening. I want to be happy and I want a real home. I have never had a real home with people who care about me."

Linda laid her hand on Laurel's arm. "You know I believe we find a place for a reason. I know I did. You might think it was awful being left behind, but look where you are now."

Laurel looked up at the sparkling white domes of the house, the wide terraces and balconies and the unbelievable blue-green views of the lake and hills, and replied softly , "This must be what heaven looks like. If you need me I can stay as long as you want." Impulsively, Linda hugged her.

"This is a beautiful country, and I am sure you will like it here. This is going to be good for both of us."

Chapter 45

LET'S GET GROWING

Lola, now being called Laurel, wrapped herself deeper into the blankets before opening her eyes and remembered where she was. It was still dark and she was excited about starting the day. Her head was full of things to do in the unbelievable job she had been offered. She needed to walk around the house, look over the grounds, talk to Linda about what she wanted and then make a plan. She needed paper and a pencil. After throwing on her clothes, she pulled a jacket out of her backpack and stood on the patio. In her jacket pocket she was delighted to find her bank check from the orphanage. She could see the black mountain peaks at the end of the lake against a red orange sky. In a moment the sun burst through the jagged hills and it was day. Sighing in appreciation, she turned to the left behind her and began to walk up the slight hill, pleased to find a mature avocado tree. Just past it on a level area she dug into the ground with her hands, and closed her fists over the dirt,, crushing and smelling it. Walking past the front door, she stepped out into the street gazing at the majestic beauty of the huge white house. Around the other side the sun was bright, and again she picked up dirt with both hands. Linda noticed her through the open kitchen window.

"Come in, I have tea ready. You are probably starving and I made muffins."

The door to the kitchen was shaded by a small arbor, and as Laurel stood taking off her shoes, she could imagine it covered with a fragrant flowering vine.

"Thanks, I can't remember what I ate yesterday. I was walking around to see what the yard looks like. It's a great setting. It could be made really beautiful."

"That's what you are going to do, Laurel. It may take a while. I still can't believe you came along just at the right time."

Through bites of muffin, Laurel mumbled, "I saw the sunrise this morning. It just blew me away. I've never seen anything like it. Can I tell you something? You are the one who came along at the right time, for me. I want to stay here and work for you if you will have me. Can you walk around the yard with me? I need to know what you want and I need a pencil and paper to draw out a plan."

Linda stood, "I have some things to do, phone calls to make first. I want to find out when the truck is coming. Let me show you where a shower is so you can wash off the road dust and start fresh. I put some garden clothes of mine in there that should fit and we can put all yours in the washer."

"Thanks, I must look like a dog's breakfast. I did find my check from the orphanage. At least Stan missed that. I'll need to figure out how to cash it."

For the next few hours, their two heads were bent close together, one smoothly dark blond and one short, red and spiky. They went over the yard and patios foot by foot, Laurel furiously scribbling the plan on paper for color and type of plant for each area.

Laurel tapped the pencil against her teeth, "What about the front of the house? I see a palm tree on each side of the walk up by the house and a hedge separating the parking lot from the front yard."

Linda Lou clapped her hands, "Oh – Yes, that would be perfect. I like your idea of a salad garden outside my kitchen door too. Do you know what you want from the garden shop to start?" Linda heard the truck before she saw it,

"Here comes the truck with the first load of what we ordered. For right now we can put everything under the front patio where the workshop is. Maybe you should go back with them and pick out anything more that you need. When they come back with those, then they can unload everything and put things in place for you."

Chapter 46

I KNOW ABOUT DIRT

Laurel's first visit to the acreage known as Garden World was a big surprise. There were acres of plants seemingly jumbled together as far as you could see. She would never know where to look to find what she wanted. . Out of the greenhouse came a kid, a funny looking kid with reddish blond hair combed to a peak on top of his head, freckles covering his face and hands.

"Can I help you?"

"I'm Laurel, from the 'La Casa Blanca Bed and Breakfast'. I have a list of things I need to buy to put in the yard."

The kid looked at the list intently and snorted, "Humph. This is pretty big stuff. Do you know what you are doing?"

Feeling insulted, Laurel pulled herself up to her four foot eleven inches and replied hotly,

"Yes, I do. If you don't have these things, I will go somewhere else."

A wry grin spread across the freckles, "Settle down, little girl, we have all this…and more…and there isn't any other place. By the way, my name is Kelly. My folks own this place. Tell me what you have in mind and we can go from there."

Still feeling prickly about being called a little girl, Laurel pulled out the workup she and Linda Lou had gone over so painstakingly. Pointing to the list and then the plan, she described what plants went where. Throughout the conversation, Kelly was nodding and, making a checkmark beside each plant on her list. When she came to the garden outside the kitchen, he put a question mark.

Laurel bristled, "What's that for?"

His answer was calm, "I don't know if that's a good place for the garden."

"And why not? That's where we want it, right outside of the kitchen in the morning sun."

He tapped her arm, "Okay, okay, it might be all right. I just need some of your dirt."

"Dirt… dirt! You want some of our dirt?"

"Yes, I do. Bring me a quart jar about half full of the dirt in that spot and a different jar from the other side of the house. Mark the jars. I will tell you what you need for a garden. I know everything about dirt, little girl, everything. Just remember that."

Sighing, as if talking to a backward child, "I guess I can do that, Mr. Know it-all."

"That's what I am, because I do know it all – about plants and gardens…and dirt."

"So shall I call you, Mr. Smarty Pants?"

"The condition of my pants has nothing to do with gardening. When you get me, you get the best. Are you ready to have the plants on this list loaded on your truck?" After whistling to his two helpers, he spoke to them quietly in liquid Spanish, while he drove the truck up and down the rows. All was packed in a short time except the two palm trees.

"I'll have to bring the palm trees separately. They need to be dug and specially packed. I will bring the bill with me then. Thanks, Laurel, I'm glad to meet you. Drive slowly now."

Chapter 47

TONALA ON A SUNDAY – 1983

Dolores wanted bright new numbers for her motel rooms, so the place to go was the huge street market at Tonala on the east side of Guadalajara. She and her friend had a ritual of lunch near there to get ready for the long walk of a mile or more down the streets of the marketplace. The vendor displays of glass and crystal, painted crafts, pictures, paintings, furniture, candles, garden supplies, plants and novelties, with headstones and birdbaths were jammed next to one another as far as the they could see. Colorful ceramic dishes, metal embossed pitchers and vases filled the eyes. One young man was selling hubcaps next to a silver jewelry stall. Dolores heard the deep, rolling laugh before she saw the man at his vendor's stall. She could see he was watching as she came down the street. She had noticed him on other occasions as she walked by his gorgeous brown and creamy gold vases, animal figures and pottery. On one occasion, he had even invited her to his house to watch him make his pottery.

Laughing, she had replied, "Not this time, I am with my friend in her car."

His quiet reply was, "Then next time come alone."

Two weeks later, on the pretense of buying a statue for the yard, she went again to the street market. That morning she had loosened her hair out of its usual tight bun, brushing it until it shone. She wore an attractive lace blouse and had dotted a few drops of cologne behind her ears. When she walked up to him, he said,

"I have been waiting for you."

She picked up one of his striking vases as he came to her, towering over her. His scent of sweet tobacco and a woodsy fragrance filled her nose. Taking the vase from her before she could speak, he drew her hand to his lips. His mouth was warm and moist, lingering on her hand. Dolores closed her eyes for a moment and a tiny tremor of pleasure ran through every part of her, leaving her shaken.

He was a big man, with silver grey hair thick around his head like a lion's mane, and braided down his back. Barrel-chested with huge shoulders and arms, browned from the sun, muscular from hard work, even his hands were as large as rocks. His fingers were those of an artist, long and slender with odd, spatulate fingernails. He threw his head back in joy when he laughed, that huge, whole hearted laugh. His features were angular: a strong nose and sparkling brown eyes, white teeth in a large mouth.

" I am Paulo Escobar. Come sit in the shade. I have something to say." She followed him as he sat her in a chair and pulled his chair close, speaking in a low voice,

"I have seen you. I have watched you. You are a beautiful woman. May I say something? I have hoped you would come back and I waited. I would like to know more about you. I want you to know who I am. This is hard for me to say but I must think what to say. My wife has been gone ten years and I am alone now. My son and family live outside the city. My daughter was just married last year and has a gift shop in Chapala. I have a great longing for a partner, a woman, to work with me and be with me. I am not young, but I have a long life in front of me. What I mean to say is, will you come home with me? Let me show you my home and my shop. We will eat, talk and get to know each other. I will bring you back here."

Dolores was moved as he spoke. She listened and looked into his eyes and found no deception or falseness. "I have noticed you as well. I like what I see. We could go to your house, just to eat and come right back, as friends, getting to know each other." A current of energy and anticipation flowed through her as she stood.

He quickly motioned to the young man in the next stall, "If you please, would you watch my shop for me while I go home for lunch?"

They drove silently to his home hidden behind a high, creamy colored wall. Opening the door, they entered into a spacious courtyard open to the blue sky, crammed with plants and flowers of all colors, geraniums and aloe, orchids and ferns and water dripping from multicolored pots. Her first impression was of pillars, short and tall ones, leading to an open stained glass door of the living quarters.

Paulo explained, "My house girl, Ana, comes in the afternoon to clean and water. She makes lunch for me and then goes home. It smells as if she has been baking. Let us see what she has for us."

The young girl, shy at first, served chicken empanadas, fruit salad and fresh rolls, warm from the oven in the shaded patio. Their conversation flowed, as Dolores was interested to know how long he had been working in pottery and when he opened his stall in the market. After she mentioned she owned a motel, he was appreciative of her hard work and day to day activity and upkeep. Lunch was over too soon.

"Let me show you my house."

Dolores was overwhelmed with the graciousness of the house; the main level was dotted with beautiful paintings, religious pictures, vases and life size animal figures. There was a huge kitchen, a guest room with a bath, as well as his study on the main level. In the airy second floor was a comfortable loft at the top of the stairs with a fireplace, and two large bedrooms, each with their own bath.

After returning to the kitchen to say goodbye to Ana, they went outside. In the yard against the back wall there was a small building that was his workshop and his kiln. She was surprised by his hobby of growing orchids, grafting and pollinating for new and striking colors. Vigorous blooming splashes of color covered a bamboo wall with an intricate network of watering lines.

He put his arm around her shoulder, "You see, you could stay and watch me work tonight."

It took a few moments for her to answer, "I will, some day."

This was the beginning of a courtship lightly designed as a friendship. Every Sunday from that day, Dolores would leave the motel about noon, leaving Maigret or Ramon at the desk. She would sit with Paulo in his vendor's space, eat with him at his home and stay to help him pack up his stall at night. They would talk and laugh. He would talk and she would listen, then she would talk and he would listen. He told her of his life, his family, his son Vincente, and his daughter, Carla, his work, the names of the colors, the different styles of sculptors. His father, a maintenance worker, had saved money for Paulo to go to college to become an engineer. His artistic abilities won out, and by luck he was invited to study under a famous potter to become trained in his skill and traditions. Dolores in turn described her life of working at the motel since she was very young, then inheriting it from her parents. The smiles, the touches, the chaste embrace and kiss goodbye became an innocent habit. She stayed later and later each visit. One Sunday about six months later, as it was starting to rain, Paulo decided to pack up early and go home for their meal.

"Ana, Anita, we are home." The house was silent. In the kitchen, they found a warm casserole dish and tortillas in a straw basket next to it. The yellow piece of paper next to them said simply,
"Mama sick. Left now."

Dolores cleared the table after their meal, seeing Paulo watch her when he thought she was not looking. "That was delicious, Paulo. You are lucky to have such a good cook."

"Come to the patio, Dolores, it has stopped raining. Sit beside me while I have a cigar. What do you think about us? Could this be the day you stay and watch me work? I have a hunger that is not for food. I have a need for you." He laid the cigar down slowly and put his arms around her, drawing her tightly to him. His body felt warm and strong against her. Their kiss was long and enjoyable. He whispered.

"Stay with me tonight, be my wife tonight."

Her whispered answer was sincere, "Yes, I will; it is time."

He made love to her with great tenderness. His touch was light and sure. They fit together like two missing pieces of a puzzle. She, tall and slim, and he, a giant of a man surrounded her. When they could wait no longer, he entered her slowly, and then was still. Dolores made a small sound and they moved together like long time lovers. When his shout of release came, she realized it was her name he was calling and thrilled to her own climax. Dolores laid her head back on the pillow with a feeling of fierce pride that she was able to create such emotion in this very special man.

They went to his church the next Sunday and arranged for the priest to marry them in Paulo's courtyard in December.

Chapter 48

BIG PLANS

Fernando and Linda had invited Dolores Diaz, friend and owner of the motel, to walk through the soon-to-be La Casa Blanca Bed and Breakfast to give them the benefit of her knowledge and experience. They walked slowly through each room studying the construction plans for the building. As the suggestions came, Fernando wrote quickly on his pad.

"A small counter would be good right inside the front door for your appointment book. You could have marble tile in the entry and hall through the dining room. Carpet would be best in the common room leading to the upstairs deck. If you took down the wall of the storage room it would open to the bathroom and then you would have two bedrooms with a bath between, good for families.

"No cooking anywhere. Just put a sink and refrigerator in the common room close to all upstairs bedrooms. Then you could have tables, couch and chairs for all to use and just a coffee maker for residents and their visitors.

"Think about building two long concrete benches on either side of the patio doors that face the lake and cover them with lots of huge, soft pillows. The apartment behind the kitchen is a good size. You might want a new refrigerator and do some painting. You can do that Linda. You probably have colors in mind."

Measurements were taken and when the three were finished, they had made good decisions. They stepped out on the second floor patio to rest a moment and enjoy the wide open view. They heard the truck grinding up the hill. Looking over they could see Kelly and Miguel unloading bushes and small trees. Laurel was directing where they should go; some were put beside holes that had already been dug.

Fernando took his wife's hand in his, "This is really going to happen. I think that when we get our first customer, we should have some kind of a party, tapas and drinks and invite all our friends."

Dolores said easily, "I wish you the best of luck."

She turned to leave then smiled, and spoke shyly, "I want to tell you something. I want you to know that I met a man last year I would like you to know better. His name is Paulo Escobar. He is – we are, what I mean to say is, we are planning to marry and I would be happy if you both would come to our wedding reception – and I need to order a big cake."

Chapter 49

A FAIRYLAND OF LIGHTS

Dolores told Paulo she needed to go to her motel the day before the wedding to tie up some loose ends and pick up her dress.

She rummaged through her closet looking for the dusty box. Opening it, she took out her mother's lace wedding dress, yellowed with age. Trying it on she was sorry, but not surprised to find that it was too small and too short. After carefully removing each band of lace, she washed them, laying them in the sun. They dried to a lovely creamy shade. Selecting a plain linen dress with a square neck, her nimble fingers carefully sewed the lace starting at the hem one layer over another up to the neckline, and then trimmed the neck and sleeves. Packing it in tissue paper, she added an ivory belt and her favorite aunt's long loop of pearls.

She listened to the everyday noises, the clip clop of a horse and rider on the highway, the hum of conversations from the restaurant patio and a chicken's low chuckle as if the egg was a surprise, thinking that the next day her life would be changed forever. She would miss this place but was happy and grateful to be marrying Paulo. She would have a home and family – everything she had wanted. She never thought there would be a great love like this for her. Knocking on Rosa's door, she gave her a note for Ramos. She and Ramos had slowly taken over the care of the motel and yard work.

The only thing left was to visit the hairdresser to find a new look for her new life.

All of Paulo's family waited quietly on the patio amidst a circle of vivid lavender, white and deep purple orchids grown by Paulo. Pots of fragrant flowers of every hue, upright scarlet geraniums, butter yellow marigolds, with moist green ferns complimenting trumpets of star gazer lilies, bent in the wisps of wind as if breathing. Every bush and tree was covered with twinkling nights. One sidewall of the yard was covered with rough stones embedded with bright pieces of pottery over which a tumbling silvery waterfall ended in the pinkness of a giant clamshell. Beside the waterfall was an impressive three foot mask done in colors of gleaming gold, chocolate brown and cream - the signature colors of Paulo's pottery ware.

The wedding was to begin at sunset. The lights and flowers made it all look like a fairyland. Ana had come early to house clean and prepare a long table of finger foods. She poured slim glasses of champagne for the family waiting for the priest. After a short sweet ceremony, all packed in their cars, music blaring from the radios, driving and honking loudly to the mariachi restaurant in Tlaquepaque.

Maigret had made two huge sheet cakes, one chocolate with strawberry filling and one creamy white bordered with lavender frosting orchids. She and Linda had brought them to the wedding dinner. Invitations had rippled through the vendors, and to friends and neighbors to join them for a wedding reception, dinner music, and of course dancing.

At about the time the wedding was taking place, a long black Lincoln town car with Texas plates pulled up in front of the Casa Redondo motel. A short stocky man got out and went in. He asked Ramos if Number 3 was available for the night.

"Yes, you can have that one."

The man opened the trunk and tugged out two huge bundles of bright yellow terry cloth towels.

"My name is Nate – I work in hotel supplies. I brought these down for Dolores. Is she coming back tonight?"

Smiling and shaking his head, Ramos replied, "No, I don't think so."

"Will she be here tomorrow?"

"No, I don't think she will be here tomorrow either. I'm the manager now."

Looking concerned, Nate queried, "Is she sick?"

Ramos looked at his watch, "No, not sick. I think right about now she is getting married."

"Married? Isn't that kind of sudden?"

"Well no, I guess they have known each other for about a year."

Nate's jaw dropped and he turned into the room, grabbed one of the bundles of towels, and threw it in the trunk, slamming the lid hard.

"I think my plans have changed. I can just make it to my next stop in Chapala. I'll leave that bundle for her – a wedding present"

Ramos gave him a big smile, "I think she'd like that."

Nate gunned the car, speeding around the half circle spewing gravel on the turn, and stopped briefly to shout out the window, "And tell her my route has changed!"

Holding back his laughter until the shiny black car disappeared in the distance to a discordant chorus of roof dogs marking his departure, Ramos declared aloud, "I think she would like that too."

Chapter 50

DANCING AND CAKE

The wedding reception was turning into a great party. Many of the vendors and friends of Paulo had come and brought their families. Ana brought her mother, and Maigret and Linda brought the cakes which were well received. Everyone danced to the festive music, even the children. Paulo danced with Dolores, then with his daughter, and with great affection, his three year old granddaughter, smiling and whispering.

Paulo got up from the table suddenly as an old man, bent over his cane, came through the archway. A younger man very similar in looks was helping him. With great care, he settled his father at Paulo's table.

Paulo laid his hand on the old man's shoulder, "My Amigo, my teacher. I am honored. Thank you for coming. This is my wife, Dolores Escobar Diaz, and this is my family. Everyone, this is my teacher who taught me all that I know and made me see his passion. He is the reason I have my work and all that is life to me. Everything I have today, I owe to him. I toast to you, Francisco." They huddled with heads together as Dolores was swept away for dance after dance, to the enthusiastic music. Maigret danced and Linda danced too.

Francisco, with his head close, explained to Paulo that he had not been teaching for several years and was getting too old to manage his storefront shop, but before he gave it up, he wanted to speak to Paulo. He spoke in an unsteady voice, saying that Paulo was his favorite of his many students over the years and that he thought only of him to do what he had in mind. He offered to turn over the rest of the lease contract to Paulo if he wanted the store in the street market of Tlaquepaque. Paulo was struck silent with gratitude. It would mean moving all of his goods, pots, dishes, figurines, everything, into a real store. It was an idea he had only dreamed of; a flush of excitement flowed through him. He could hardly wait to talk it over with Dolores.

Francisco raised a trembling hand and, in a weak but sincere voice, spoke, "I have one request."

"Anything Maestro, whatever you ask, it is done."

"Will you keep some of my pieces in a small part of the store to sell them for me? I would like to think my name will not disappear."

Paulo clapped his hands, "This is a wonderful thing you ask, to have my name next to yours. I would do this with great respect. Your name will be known for a hundred years. Thank you for this gift on my wedding day. It will not be forgotten."

Francisco waived to his son for assistance. As he rose, he embraced Paulo, "Come to my house in one week."

Dolores and Paulo talked long into the night. She knew in her heart that Paulo's gift and love of his work was something special. And so it came to be, that the name of 'Escobar' was added to the sign over the door of the store. Prominently displayed in one window was Francisco's lovely pieces and Paulo's of cream and gold were displayed in the other window. The store was large with a comfortable sitting room in the back and Dolores could be there with him at the store. Over time, Dolores grew to be friends with the woman next door and accepted sewing and alterations from her clothing store. Paulo and Dolores were happy together and their business flourished.

Chapter 51

ALMOST OPEN

The two palm trees had just been deposited in the holes prepared by the front door, planted and smoothed over when a taxi drove into the parking lot, crunching on the gravel. The driver unloaded several bulky bags, staggering under their weight but carried them in as well as the two pet carriers.

Over a medley of barking, a loud voice was heard demanding "I'd like a room, please."

Linda came rushing down the wide stairs from the second floor, surprised and a little confused, "We don't have our 'OPEN' sign out yet. We're still painting upstairs."

"I don't want to be upstairs, I need to be on the main level, walking you know," she said, as she shook a cane in the air. "I don't mind the smell of paint. I am here and not going anywhere else. What's the rate for a week?"

Quickly, Linda opened her daybook on the counter and pretended to read it. The sudden appearance of this tall, imposing woman in clothes from a bygone era, dripping with beads and chains, more than slightly surprised her.

"Yes, we do have a room, just one on this floor. Actually, it is two rooms with a bath between. If you'd like both rooms, it's a bit more."

"I'm Mrs. Mather, Beulah Mather, and these are my children, my mini dachshunds, Betty, she's the mother, and Hutton, she's the daughter. Two rooms would be better than one, so they can have one for themselves. They snore, you know. Whatever your rate is will be just fine. I'd like to stay for a week. I was told you have one of the best views on the lake. That's really what I want."

Linda marked the book for seven days, giving Mrs. Mather a copy of the receipt showing the dates, the rate and a Saturday departure. "We have a very nice breakfast every day, except Sunday. You can have it in your room, here in this room, or on the patio. Just let me know. Checkout is at noon. Let me get someone to help with your luggage. Thank you for coming. How did you know about us?"

"Oh, my friend in Chapala told me. She said to just look for the big white house on the top of the hill."

The week went by and the painting was finally finished. It seemed as if Mrs. Mather went somewhere every day with her small dogs leading her. She had inquired about staying for one more day. After breakfast on Saturday, all the workers had gone and Laurel went back to the casita, when Linda heard car doors slam. The sound of people coming up the walk and the car doors roused Linda from a brief nap on the patio. The gentleman was holding a lady under her arm as she hobbled in the front door.

"Hello, I'm Carl Day and this is Elizabeth, Liz for short. We were wondering if you have a room. My wife sprained her ankle walking on the cobblestones yesterday and they told us at the clinic that you have a main floor room. We are in the motel on the highway, but we are on the second floor. She would rather not go up and down stairs."

Linda looked disappointed, "I wish we did. The room you want has someone in it right now who might stay over until tomorrow. I am so sorry about your ankle. Please, rest a little outside on the patio. I can bring you some tea or coffee." The phone rang and interrupted her trip to the patio with the refreshments. The call was for Mrs. Mather; Linda knocked on her door as she went by, telling her the phone at the front desk was for her.

Mrs. Mather appeared on the patio, seeming somewhat agitated. "The pups and I are going on a boat ride today from the pier, so I guess I won't be staying over. Would you call me a taxi, please?"

Linda called over the patio to Laurel in the casita to come up and help with the luggage, and Mr.

Day went hurrying down to the highway to check out of their two story lodgings.

When Laurel came back into the room, the two women did a little dance and hugged each other. Linda tapped on the glass over the wedding picture of Bernie and Harlan.

"Our first customer Bernie - and a second one soon."

Chapter 52

LA CASA BLANCA

Linda and Fernando walked hand in hand through the rooms of their home. The new and shiny 'OPEN' sign was in place. All rooms were colorful, and newly painted, with attractive furniture they had selected, and beds that were fresh and appealing with elegant comforters, breathtaking pictures on the walls, beautiful vases ready for flowers and, best of all, a wedding picture of Harlan and Bernice just inside the front door. Linda patted the picture as she passed. The grounds were impeccable, a lush invitation for visitors to enter and lose themselves in the grassy walkways of tropical plants, arbors, and fragrant and wildly colorful flowering bushes. Two wrought iron benches sat on the point of the yard facing the magnificent panorama of the lake under a flourishing trellis of purple passionflowers. The two palm trees stood tall and dignified on each side of the front door, waiting for the new era to begin.

"Well, Linda, are you happy with how everything turned out?"

In a hushed voice, Linda replied, "This is so much more than I ever dreamed of. Bernice would be so pleased. This couldn't have happened without you, my love."

"You know it was both of us. Now we have to sit down and plan our Open House. We need people to know we are here and are open. I'll get paper and a pencil. Let's sit out on the patio and look at our lake. First, I will contact the newspaper. I think they can print us our business cards too."

"We will need food and flowers. Juana can make us an appetizer buffet and Maigret will be able to make a big cake. Do you want to have anything to drink?"

Fernando shook his head, "I think coffee and tea would be enough, and maybe juice. I would want it to be in the middle of day when the lake is at its best. I'll ask Laurel to get flowers and she can choose some potted plants for the two patios."

"I think it would be nice if there was music…would Ruby play for us?"

Fernando grinned, "Good idea, I am sure she will. I also thought about asking the sketch artist in the plaza to come up for a few hours and do sketches of our visitors. What do you think?

Linda clapped her hands, "Oh yes, I want one of us too. Could we have prizes? People love prizes. We could give away a weekend stay. This is going to be such a good time. Are we finished? I have an idea for us for lunch."

Fernando took her hands in his, kissing them, "We are ready for business. This part is over, and I have my own idea for lunch."

They stood arm in arm looking with satisfaction at the stunning waters of the lake.

Linda sighed, "It's always there isn't it? So dependable. So beautiful. Sometimes I have to pinch myself to see if all this is real. You know, this all started with Harlan and Bernie. If it weren't for them and for me meeting Bernie, none of this would have happened. I just wish they could see how perfect it has turned out. Fernando looped his arms around her waist from behind, resting his chin on her hair.

"Somehow I think they know. Some way, somehow, I just think they know."

The two heads in the wedding picture on the wall behind them turned to each other and the white haired man patted his wife's hand and gave her a grin and a big wink.

THE END

ACKNOWLEDGEMENTS

There are so many people who helped this book form and grow. To mention a few, in the very beginning from Judy E, who gave me the germ of an idea from a popular saying about 'The Dust of Mexico'. My first proof readers Sally F., Sheila K., Judith C., and of course Joe.

Laurette R., who lent me her home in Chula Vista, Mexico to begin. Wende M., who gave me all of her Writers' Digest books and class notes. Diane O. for continuing online classes, newsletters and seminars. Mary B., for her seminar "Sex Between the Pages".

To my New York critique and professional correction agent, Jolene P., who read every line and did a magnificent job.

To my husband Joseph Guadalupe Torres, for packing every suitcase on our thirty or more trips throughout Mexico.

Most of all to Judy King, who first believed in my writing for her online magazine mexico-insights.com. She continually supported and encouraged me. She brought Betty W. to my attention to format and polish. Betty directed me to a photographer for the cover and they both pointed out items for me to make decisions so it could then move smoothly onto the printed page.

I am forever grateful.
Carolena Torres

Carolena Torres is a native Oregonian who has had the good fortune to travel several dozen times to different parts of Mexico. She is a singer, guitar player and author of articles published in the online magazine, *Living at Lake Chapala*, about her visits to many areas of Mexico. She is married to Joseph Torres who has been her companion in these travels and her biggest fan.

A good friend and B&B owner repeated to her the saying made popular by Neill James of Ajijic, "When the dust of Mexico falls upon your heart, you will never be the same." And, the dust did fall on her heart and the idea of this, her debut novel, began to build.

www.ingramcontent.com/pod-product-compliance
Lightning Source LLC
Chambersburg PA
CBHW020341180626
46812CB00001B/296